NO TURNING BACK

NO TURNING BACK

Hemalatha Gnanasekar

KALPAZ

No Turning Back

ISBN : 978-81-7835-943-4

Published in 2013 in India by
Kalpaz Publications
C-30, Satyawati Nagar,
Delhi - 110052
E-mail: kalpaz@hotmail.com

Laser Type Setting : Rajender Vashist, Delhi
Printed at : G. Print Process,Delhi

Dedicated to
Shirdi Sai Baba
for His blessings

Preface

It has been rightly said that the best gift a father can give to his children is to love their mother. The relationship between parents do impact the growth and development of a child and parent rivalry is sure to have adverse effects. Nowadays, with multi-tasking, parents are always on a tight schedule which makes them less tolerant and more impatient. They are all the time anxious, worried or unhappy and are unable to have a hold on their emotions. For a relaxed life, they need to cultivate patience and move towards peace by being kind and generous in forgiveness of others. Otherwise, it would result in the end of a relationship that is most important to you.

In "No Turning Back", Swaminathan too is a victim of parent rivalry. Ever since his childhood, he had grown up seeing his parents quarrel with each other almost every other day. Unable to bear his father's harsh words, his mother leaves the house one day; only to end her life. On learning about this, his father is traumatised so much so that he too ends his life impulsively. Having lost both his parents on the same day, Swaminathan moves to his aunt's house where he gets all the love. This makes him take a drastic decision in his life that if he ever marries, he would treat his wife with deep live and kindness. But as Fate would have it, Swaminathan is married to Shanthi who turns out to be of a nit picking character. Her nagging slowly gets on Swaminathan's nerves and he is now gripped with constant fear if he would also turn out to be violent like his father. A malicious act on her part makes Swaminathan so wild and he walks out of her life one day; without as much as word to anyone. Many years later, Ramanathan, a family friend of Shanthi bumps into him and is shocked beyond beliefs at the life Swaminathan is leading. Being a Philanthrophist, he is now bent on uniting the couple and tries to change Swaminathan's mind? Does Ramanathan succeed in his endeavour?

"No Turning Back" is a short novel intended for those women out there who take their husbands for granted and wish to boss over them. They continuously keep carping at them; wishing to have the last word always. The book is a warning to these nagging women; for the angry outbursts of their henpecked husbands could get them no where. They better make haste in amending themselves in order to lead a smooth and peaceful marital life.

Hemalatha Gnanasekar

No Turning Back

Ramanathan gingerly opened the cover and took out a handful of puffed rice flakes. Absent mindedly he started dropping them little by little into the water. He saw the fishes gather up around it. They nibbled at the rice flakes and greedily gobbled them up. *He had met the man before. His face seemed to be very familiar. But he could not recall his name nor did he have any cue as to where he had met him.* Racking his brains about the man he had just seen, Ramanathan continued scattering the rice flakes until he realised that the cover was empty.

Ramanathan was Fifty Five years old. After his voluntary retirement, he spent his time by doing social service. This gave him peace of mind and a sense of fulfillment in life. Slowly, the news about his helping nature got around and people came to him and confessed their problems. Ramanathan was quick to offer his valuable advice and suggestions to them. At times, he even went out of his way to find a solution to their woes ; be it obtaining a seat in a school or college, finding a suitable marriage alliance for their children, settlement of disputes between spouses or bringing to end the petty quarrels on the streets either between children or the grownups. When people lauded him for his philanthrophic activities, he would simply say, "to God be the praise. I am but an instrument of His !"

In the beginning of every New Year, Ramanathan went on a short pilgrimage to obtain the blessings of God. This year, he came to Kanchipuram. He had finished his visit to all the temples and finally landed up in the Kacchapaeswarar Temple. At the entrance there is a small Vinayaga Temple. Ramanathan entered the temple to obtain the blessings of Lord Vinayaga. He stood there among the crowd praying as the young priest was chanting the mantras. And when at last Ramanathan received the prasad from the priest, he was startled. The face of the man looked very familiar and he at once realised he had met him earlier. But only Ramanathan was not sure, where he had met him. Being Sankata Chaturthi, the temple was very crowded and the man was rather busy. Wishing to clear his doubts later on, Ramanathan decided to come round the Sanctum Sanctorum. After making three rounds, he felt tired and hence sat down on the steps of the cool water tank at the entrance of the temple.

While he kept brooding about the familiar face, he cursed his poor memory, which was of late, failing him and messing up his life. He decided, it was high time that he did something about it. But right now, his curiosity got the better of him and he was bent upon knowing more about the priest. He stood up and started walking slowly in his direction.

Ramanathan waited patiently for the crowd to disperse. At last, when he found the priest alone, he went up to him and said, "your face seems to be very familiar to me. I remember having met you somewhere. Are you from Chennai ?" Astonished that somebody recognised him, the priest nodded his head and said, "I am from Baskara Street in West Mambalam."

Ramanathan's face brightened up and he continued, "I live in the adjoining street of yours. And by the way, may I know your name please ?"

Irked by the oldman's nosiness, the priest said, "My name is Swaminathan."

With this curt reply, he made a move from there to waive camphour to God for the people who had just entered the temple.

Creasing up his forehead, Ramanathan continued, "are you by any chance Shanthi's husband ?"

Jolted by his question, Swaminathan retreated his steps.

"Yes, of course ! But how do you know that ?" He asked with bewilderment.

Ramanathan was excited. For once, his memory has not let him down. Beaming with a smile, he said, "well, I know Shanthi very well. She used to come to me for Maths Tuition. I also attended your marriage function and I remember Shanthi having introduced me to you. Perhaps you might have forgotten it!"

Swaminathan stood there grinning sheepishly, anticipating his next question, when the old man continued, "are you not staying with your family ?"

At first, Swaminathan did not appreciate the old man's probing nature. But when he told him that he knew his wife too well, he was eager to strike a conversation with him. He was rather amazed with the keen interest the old man evinced in him and so he blurted out rather coyly, "well, I am no more staying with her. We could not get along with each other and I have left her for good six years back!"

Ramanathan was disappointed to hear this. It is only now that things were becoming clear as daylight to him. For whenever he had chanced to meet Shanthi on the way, he had found her in a depressed mood. She was not her usual self. And whenever he had enquired about her husband, she would simply say that he was doing fine. After this, she would either try to change the subject or make an attempt to leave. Perplexed as to what could be the misunderstanding that had cropped up between the couple that has resulted in their separation, Ramanathan asked, "would you care to tell me the reasons for your leaving her ?"

Swaminathan was silent.

Ramanathan was quick to notice the hestitation on his face and he said, "hope you are not upset about my prying you with questions. Since I know Shanthi very well, I am just anxious to know the cause of your separation."

A small crowd had already gathered there and Swaminathan excused himself, "I am afraid this is not the right place to talk about it. If you don't mind, could you please meet me tonight. I would rather be too willing to open out my heart to you then."

Ramanathan took out a small sheet of paper and jotted down his address and promised to visit him. Here was an opportunity for him to do something good and he was too excited about it.

Swaminathan rushed inside to renew his puja and as he waived camphour to God, he wondered as to what could be God's purpose in bringing this old man to him !

Ramanathan had in fact finished his round of temples. He had been planning to leave for Chennai immediately after visiting Kacchapaeswarar Temple. But now, he changed his mind and extended his stay in the hotel for another day. He went to his room and had a good sleep. When he woke up, it was already 7.30 p.m. He hurriedly had his dinner and started walking to Swaminathan's house ; making sure that he had the small bit of paper in which he had noted down his address.

He was able to easily locate Swaminathan's house. But when he found it locked, his spirits fell. He sat down on the steps and decided to wait for him. The compact house very much resembled his own at Chennai. Ramanathan sat there reminiscing the past. A few years ago, his only son and daughter-in-law, settled in Bangalore, had requested him to join them. But Ramanathan had curtly refused by telling that he did not wish to intrude their privacy nor be a burden to them. With the lump sum money he received at the time of retirement, he purchased an old and dilapidated house and renovated it. Though it was a very small house, his wife liked it because it was an independent house. However, she was upset that he had turned down the request of his son and daughter-in-law ; for she missed them a lot. Ramanathan had pacified her by promising to take her to Bangalore every year during the summer vacation, when she could happily spend her time with her grand children. Just before Ramanathan started for Kanchipuram, a place which is well known for its temples and silk sarees, she had requested him to buy a silk saree to gift it to her daughter-in-law and he had assented for the same. Seeing that Swaminathan had still not arrived, he wished to finish off his shopping first. Just as he got up, he saw Swaminathan coming in a bike.

"Today being Sankatahar Chaturthi, the temple was very crowded and hence the delay", Swaminathan apologised as he got down from the bike.

Ramanathan smiled and silently followed him in. He was rather surprised to note that the house was nothing but one large room which Swaminathan had prudently partitioned. It into a kitchen, bedroom and a hall. Finding no chairs around, Ramanathan sat down on the bed in the corner of the room. He heard some cluttering of vessels and within a few minutes, he saw Swaminathan enter with a plate holding two cups of coffee. After offering one to Ramanathan, he helped himself with one and sat down on the floor after spreading a mat. Appreciating the good coffee, Ramanathan too came and sat down beside him on the mat and reclined on the wall.

There was just silence hanging in the air for sometime as both men kept sipping their coffee. At last Swaminathan broke the ice, "I am sorry to have kept you waiting for so long. Though I intended to be here by 7.30 p.m, people kept coming in and I could not close the temple early."

"That's o.k. There is no problem. Afterall, I am a retired man and have got all the time in this world. But to be frank, it is you whom I really pity. You are a young man and it pains my heart to know that you are not staying with your wife and daughter. You have come down here after abandoning your hi-fi job and family. I wonder what has made you get so disheartened with your family. Perhaps you could have been too angry with your wife, but what has your poor daughter done to you ? Are you not responsible for her well being ? Whatever be the cause, I do not approve of your leaving your family in the lurch and strongly denounce your impulsive action."

Swaminathan was hurt by his overbearing words and he said, "I respect the regard you have for my wife and daughter. But I am rather cut up with your rebuff. In the first place, I wish to clarify to you that it is for my loving daughter that I had forsaken everything and come over here. It would indeed be very kind of you if you could lend me your ears and listen to me patiently for sometime. I had been longing to share my inner feelings with someone and seek justification as to whether the decision I had taken in my life is right or wrong. For eversince I left my family, I have been filled with a feeling of guilt. God has atlast listened to my prayers and has now sent you to me." Swaminathan then began to narrate his story :

I was the only son to my parents. It was my mother who was more affectionate towards me. My father never exhibited his love to me. I often would become jealous of my friends when they spoke highly of their father, who took them on frequent picnics, played games with them or bought them birthday presents. I too longed for my father's love. Instead, all I got from him was scoldings and beatings.

Unfortunately, being the only child, I was also the victim of my parent's frequent rivalry. Due to bad friendship, my father slowly got addicted to drinks. In the beginning, it was only during the weekends that he would come home drunk and start a fight with mother. But eventually, he started to drink everyday. For no reason, he would get furious and start yelling at mother and fling things at her. Most of the time, my mother, aware that he was intoxicated and in a booze never retaliated.

I still remember the agony and pain she went through all the years with my father. Any other woman in her place would have left him long ago. But my mother bore it all silently just for my sake. For she did not want me to grow up without a father. She also believed that father would turn over a new leaf one day or the other. But he never showed any signs of change. It was when I came to the tenth standard that I witnessed a sea change in my mother's character. Her anger grew up by leaps and bounds.

The reason for this was that my father stopped giving his salary to her. Addicted to drinks, he spent his entire salary for drinks and mother was finding it very difficult to make both ends meet. Many a nights we would go to bed starving without having dinner while my father would return home fully drunk. He would immediately lie down on the bed and start snoring even without bothering to ask us if we had our dinner or not. Mother was pained by the fact that she was not able to provide me with even one square meal per day ; especially when I was studying very hard for my tenth board examination.

One fine day, my mother discussed about this with her neighbour, who was very close to her. The kind lady advised my mother to go out for some work. She suggested that, these days there was a demand for a good cook and since my mother had a great culinary skill, she was sure to find a job. Further, through an acquaintance of hers, she found a job for my mother.

After seeking my father's permission, my mother went out to work. It was during this time that I saw some smile on my mother's face. For now, there was no dearth of food and clothing at home. Mother bought me several dresses. She also saved up some money for a few months and purchased a bicycle that I had been longing for. I rode the bicycle proudly to my school everyday. In fact, now she had money to buy me anything that I asked for.

On the other hand, my father started to envy her. The fact that she was leading an independent life without caring much for him was getting on his nerves. One Sunday morning, he went out early in the morning. He returned after a heavy drink. When he saw my mother getting ready to go out, he told her that there was no necessity for her to go out and work. My mother argued with him that since he was not giving her a single pie, she had no other alternative but to go out and work. Enraged by her rude rejoinder, he at once slapped her. Further, he threatened her that if she stepped out of the house, he would throw her out for ever.

My mother had turned very courageous indeed. For, to my surprise, she did not get cowed down by his threats this time. Boldly, she retorted that she needed money to run the household and educate her son and hence she was going out for work. She also blamed him that it was due to his uncaring attitude that she was forced to work and that no one can stop her from going to work. With these words, she made a move from there. But immediately, father dragged her in and started hitting her. Crying aloud, my mother told him that if he did not allow her to work, she was going to walk out of his life for ever. At this, father's anger raised further and he told her to get lost.

My mother quickly entered the bed room and started dumping a few clothes into a bag. She came out, cursing my father under her breath. Holding my hand, she walked out of the door.

Father ordered me to stop. But I continued walking along with my mother. Suddenly, he came and stood in front of my mother blocking our way. He started yelling at her again, "I don't care even if you go and hang yourself. But don't ever think of taking my son along with you. From this moment you don't have any right over him !" He started dragging me towards him but mother held me tight and did not let me go. I was being pulled by both my parents as though I was a rope in a game of tug of war.

At last my mother gave in. She started to beg him, "you hardly have any time for your son. You have sent him to bed many a nights without food. You had money for your drinks but when I asked you to buy provisions, you always refused under one pretext or other. And if I leave my son under your care, I am sure that you would starve him to death. I am the right Guardian for him. So, please let him go with me."

But father was in no mood to listen to her pleadings. He slapped me hard and asked me to get into the house. Whimpering in pain, I requested mother to leave me and entered the house ; scared that father would hit me again if I did not obey him. My mother felt humiliated over this. She knew that father was exploiting her by mistreating me. And finally she screamed "if you don't let my son to come with me, I shall end my life !"

Father only chuckled on hearing her angry words as though it were a joke and he said, "I don't care a damn for you anymore !" At his harsh words, mother started to shout at the top of her voice, "you will repent for this. This time, I am really serious. Once again, I am requesting you to send my son along with me. He is the only solace to me. If you refuse to oblige me, I am heading to the railway station this instant. You will soon see my corpse on the tracks !" But father did not care a jot for all her hollering.

Mother's temper grew skyhigh at his heartlessness. Hurling the bag into the hall, she rushed out of the house in a great huff. On seeing my mother walk briskly on the road, I started pleading with father to let me go along with her. But he denied permission and further said, "where would your mother go ? She has nowhereelse to go and after a while, she will surely come back home !"

With these words, he fell on the bed and started snoring. I too strongly believed that mother would come back home shortly. If not for my father, atleast for me! It was around 1.00 p.m when father woke up. He was now in a sober mood. Immediately he went from one room to another searching for my mother. Not finding her, he came to me and asked, "where is your mother?" When I told him that she did not come back home yet, his face changed colour.

He then left the house telling me that he would go and look around for her. He also told me that he would get something for me to eat. I was confident that somehow father would search and bring my mother back. However, as the time kept passing by, I started to panic. It was after almost two hours that father returned that too with no news of my mother. Finally when it was 4.00 p.m. he started to get terrified. Tugging me along, he walked towards the Kodambakkam railway station, which is nearby to my house. I walked silently beside him with heart in my mouth, worrying about my mother.

We walked on the platform looking around for my mother. I kept praying all the while that my mother should be alive somewhere and should have not acted in a freakish manner by ending her life in anger. As I was trying to keep pace with my father, I was rather dismayed to see a stretcher near the station master's room in which a body was covered with a cloth. I pointed it out to father who immediately hastened his steps in that direction for a closer examination.

He slowly opened the cloth. It was my mother. He started screaming aloud, running from one end of the platform to the other, beating his chest in a mad frenzy. Unable to bear the torments of my father, she had ended her life by falling in front of a train in order to revenge my father. For a second, she had forgotten all about her son and had given in to her whims.

Crying aloud for my mother, I too ran behind my father deliriously. Holding my hands, my father said amidst sobs, "I cannot live without your mother !" He kept repeating this statement over and over again. I stood there weeping and concomittantly wondering if my father really meant what he was saying. Did he care for my mother ? Did he miss her too ?

Suddenly, he abandoned me on the platform and started running. Before I could comprehend what was wrong with him, I was in for another shock. Father had seen a fast train approaching and he started running in the track in its direction. My father too ended his life along with my mother on the same day.

As two men brought the corpse of my father and lay it aside my mother's, I cried my heart out not knowing what to do. The kind Station Master came out on hearing my screams and took me in. After pacifying me, he listened patiently to my grievances. He then asked me to give him the contact number of any close relative that I knew. Immediately, I gave my maternal aunt's number.

I consider myself as the most unfortunate person in this world for having had to witness the horrific sight of losing both my parents on the same day. My mother had given vent to her anger without any concern for me. I was rather filled with anger over her foolhardy action. And I am still not sure if my father was in a booze or in a sober mood when he ended his life on that unlucky day. However on that fateful day, I had learnt an important lesson in my life - Anger could kill! I decided never to lose my temper at any cost nor hurt anybody by being rude.

I grew up in my aunt's house. My aunt, my mother's sister is a kind woman and brought me up in a loving manner. However, my uncle was a gruffy person. In the beginning, he quarrelled with my aunt frequently over my presence. Sensing his dislike for me, I tried to maintain a distance with him.

I helped my aunt by doing petty jobs for her. And at times when the servant did not turn up, I washed the vessels and clothes and swept the house. At times I also cooked meals when my aunt was sick. On seeing this, my uncle too asked me to do some shopping for him. I also carried out a few errands for him from time to time. In this way, I slowly won a place in his heart.

Immediately after completion of B.Com Degree, I got a job in a reputed company as an Accountant. The fact that I was now independent in life, gave me confidence. One fine day, my aunt opened up the subject of marriage. I told her that there was no hurry for my marriage now. I also told her that I wished to be of financial assistance to her for a few years. For in spite of paucity of funds at home, my aunt had never once complained about having to shoulder additional responsibility of taking care of me. I now wished to recompense her for all her kindness.

However, my aunt did not heed to my words. She stealthily registered my name along with details about me in several match making centres. One fine evening, when I returned from work, I saw an old man, a total stranger to me, chatting with my aunt. As I was wondering who he was, my aunt called me and introduced me to Shanthi's father.

After a brief conversation with me, he told my aunt that he was much impressed with me. Further, he invited us to his house to see his daughter. After, getting my concurrence, my aunt fixed up the marriage date immediately. I was rather upset with her for rushing up my marriage rather too soon.

My Father-In-Law transferred one of his houses that he was renting out, at Baskara Street in West Mambalam into Shanthi's name. So, immediately after marriage, I moved into my new house along with Shanthi in great happiness.

I tried very hard to erase the past from my life, which was led in great drudgery. I looked forward to a new life with great hope and promise. I took a silent vow that I shall keep Shanthi happy all my life, no matter what. I shall never raise my voice or be harsh with her. Further, I decided never to lose my temper with her. For the lesson, anger could kill was deeply ingrained in me. In fact, I decided to be everthing that my father was not - kind, loving and respectful towards my wife.

But what man proposes, God disposes. Sometimes, things don't turn out as we plan. On the very first night itself, I was in for a shock. It was 10.00 p.m, when Shanthi entered the bed room. She was looking very gloomy and there was no smile on her face. After bolting the door behind her, she straightly went and stood in front of a table with her back to me, toying with the fruits on a plate.

Wanting to start a conversation with her, I walked up to her. As I held her hand, she moved away swiftly from me. I thought that probably she was shy and scared of the first night rituals and hence was being very peevish. Once again I gently held her hand and brought her to the bed and requested her to sit down. I too sat down beside her. However, she did not look at my side and kept staring at the floor as though I did not exist in the room. Getting closer to her, I lifted her chin so that she could directly look into my face. I was dazed to see tears dripping from her eyes.

"You seem to be crying ! What's wrong?" I asked.

She did not answer me.

"You also look so pale. Are you afraid of me?" I coaxed.

She remained silent.

"Now tell me what is it you are upset about. Are you unhappy with this marriage?" I kept pestering her to speak up.

She continued to remain silent.

Not able to elicit any reply from her, at last I said, "there is no joy in your face. Don't you like me?"

"No!", she screamed at me.

Suddenly the world around me started to collapse. I could not believe what I was hearing. For a second I was not sure if she was just joking or whether she really meant it. But as her face was grim eversince she entered the room, I opined that she might probably be telling the truth.

I had faced many storms before. Perhaps marriage was the advent of another misfortune in my life. But no adversity can really make a difference in my life. I had turned hardheaded like a rock and was prepared to face any hardship in life. However, I wished to know what exactly was in her mind and so I prodded, "were you in love with someoneelse ? Or were you compelled to marry me ?"

"No !" She shook her head.

Maintaining my cool, I persisted, "there must be some valid reason for you to dislike me. Am I not entitled to know that ?"

At last she confessed the reason for being cheerless. "I am rather jealous of you ! Since you are fairer and more handsome than me, everyone were admiring you. Usually, it was me who would get second looks and people would always speak high of my beauty. But on the wedding day, I heard people say that you look more handsome than me. That's what I am really upset about !"

Her explanation for her glumness only made me laugh aloud. I then started to pacify her, "In fact, that should make you feel proud of your husband and not jealous. It is funny that you were depressed over such a trivial thing."

Continuing to pout, she said, "what if you leave me one day and go away behind some other girl ? What will become of me ? Where will I go ...."

I stopped her rumbling by placing my palm over her mouth and drew her closer to me. "I like the innocent way you talk. But let me make it clear to you that I am not such a type of person. Now stop worrying unnecessarily !" I chided her affectionately.

In order to bring her out of her sullen mood, I told her my pathetic tale of losing both my parents on the same day and landing up in my aunt's house. The story evoked pity in her for she sat there bemused listening to me with rapt attention. For a long time that night, we kept talking ; exploring each other's lives.

As days passed by, I realised that Shanthi was a hard nut to crack. While I was really feeling proud about Shanthi's possessive-ness of me, the fact that she always regarded me with an eye of suspicion perturbed me a lot.

She was so unsophisticated for she lived with a constant fear as though somebody was going to usurp her place. Despite my assurance, she mistrusted me and was apprehensive of losing her position or affection. Hence, she was always on the look out for an opportunity to find fault with me. If at all I tolerated her nagging, it was due to the resolution I had taken of not losing my temper at her. Perhaps it was this lenient nature of mine that turned her into a nitpicking and bossy woman which slowly started getting on my nerves.

However, I silently put up with everything hoping that she would turn over a new leaf in the near future when she gets a better understanding of me.

A fortnight after our marriage, when I was in office, my aunt called up. She invited us for a feast at her house and I readily agreed. I told her that we shall be coming on the following Sunday. In the evening, when I conveyed the news to Shanthi, she resented.

She told me that she was not willing to accompany me to my aunt's house. When I asked her the reason for her disgust over my aunt, whom she has hardly met, she said, "I hate all the good-for-nothing relatives. All they know is only to speak ill of others."

I then tried to convince her that my aunt is not any Tom, Dick or Harry, but my foster mother who had brought me up with loving care. In fact, she had showered more love to me than to her children. Finally I said, "I owe a lot to my aunt for the life I am leading today. While my mother had heartlessly given up her life after a fight with my father ; without any concern for me, my aunt had reared me with great love and affection."

But my justification to attend the feast at my aunt's house fell on her deaf ears and she immediately blurted, "don't keep bragging about your aunt all the time. She is one of the most cunning and selfish women I had ever known. She had in fact used you as a live-in servant maid and that too without paying you a penny."

Further, holding her palms together, she prayed, "please listen to me now ! If you truly love me, don't ever call me to that lady's house again. I don't like to visit the place, where you led your life completely at their mercy. I am sure they will extend the same treatment to me also and I don't like to be in a place where I will be looked down upon !"

Though I found myself seething with anger, I tried to restrain myself from speaking harshly.

I regretted in the first place of having revealed everything about my past life to Shanthi. For she was now using it to backfire me. But the damage had already been done and it was too late to repent. However, I did not wish to disappoint my aunt and so decided to go alone to her house.

On Sunday morning, my aunt once again reminded me about her invitation and wished to know when we would be reaching home. I lied to her that since Shanthi was not feeling well, I was coming alone. On hearing this, Shanthi came running from the kitchen and shot me a daggers look and said, "so your aunt is more important to you than me ! Despite my telling you about my hatred towards that woman, you have decided to go there for a feast, not caring for my words. Well, you are also as selfish and cunning like your aunt."

I was enraged by her arrogance and controlled my urge to hit her. She continued ranting for a long time and I sat there in grim silence not knowing what to do.

After sulking for more than half-an-hour, I went up to her and cajoled, "but for my aunt, I would have not got married to you........" Even before I completed my sentence, she butted in, "that again shows her cleverness. She wanted to wash off her hands and shun away from the responsibility of taking care of you. Marriage was just an excuse to indirectly ask you to leave the house."

Provoked by her words, I left the place in a huff. She always wanted to have the last word in an argument and I let her have it.

Before leaving the house, I went up to her and said, "it is not proper to refuse an invitation. Now that I have come to know of your hatred for my aunt, I shall in future evade going there. But let me go now ."

I did not get any reply from her. As I left the house, I heard loud cluttering noises of the vessels. I knew Shanthi was giving vent to her anger but I continued without bothering.

I was given a warm reception at my aunt's house. Everyone were upset that Shanthi did not accompany me. My aunt served me a sumptuous lunch and at the time of taking leave, she requested me to come again someother day along with Shanthi. She also handed over a small carry bag containing some vadais and payasam and asked me to give it to Shanthi.

On reaching home, I went into the kitchen first, looking for Shanthi. The kitchen was in shambles and Shanthi was not there. I then found her lying in the bed reading a book. She had probably stopped cooking the moment I left the house. In order to make peace with her, I handed over the cover my aunt gave me and said, "my aunt has offered this for you."

Without even receiving it from me, she started yelling, "so, you had had your fill in your aunt's house, without caring a pin for me. Now are you satisfied of defying me ?"

Since she had not eaten anything, I thought that she must be feeling hungry and hence was in a bad mood. I took out a vadai from the cover and said, "perhaps you had not had your lunch yet. You must be feeling hungry. Please have this."

This only added fuel to fire and she immediately burst out, "I told you I hate that aunt of yours ! Do you expect me to eat something given by her ?"

Immediately, she grabbed the carry bag from me and flung it across the room screaming, "I may rather die of hunger but never will I touch something that she has offered."

I sat there silently watching her unruly behaviour; wondering how much guts she must be having to misbehave in this manner. Gritting my teeth, I stared at her for a while and later left the place in a huff without speaking a word. I also decided not to talk to her for the rest of the day lest I lose my temper.

However, late in the evening, I realised my folly and tried to compromise with her by requesting her for a cup of coffee.

Gradually, in order to remain in her good books, I severed my ties with my aunt. I spoke to her very rarely over the phone and that too from my office.

The fact that I was completely losing my independence after marriage was a matter of distress to me. Shanthi was being too insolent and demanding day after day and it was hard to please her. My office closed at 5.30 p.m and she expected me to be at home by 6.00 p.m sharp. If due to some exigencies, I reach home late, the hell would turn loose that day. She would keep ranting for the rest of the evening that I was neglecting her. Sometimes, her harangue of words would rouse my anger and at such times, I would keep telling myself to stay calm for "anger could kill". I slowly learnt to tackle her outbursts by remaining silent without giving a rejoinder.

My boss was quick to notice the change in me. For whenever he came to my seat after 5.00 p.m. he found me missing. Scared that I would be held up in the office by my boss, I made it a point to disappear from my seat after 5.00 p.m. In the beginning, he was silent over this ; considering the fact that I was newly married. But after a few months, he was irked by this fact and one fine day he asked, "has your wife enslaved you ? Is it her instruction that you should reach home early ?"

I did not answer him but stood there grinning sheepishly.

Patting me on my back, he said, "what a nice henpecked husband you have become ?"

Once again, I gave him a broad smile and did not retort. For, I had no comments to offer for his sarcasm. Afterall, he was telling the truth.

However, this did not stop him from coming to me after 5.00 p.m. Once in a while, he would barge into my room during the fag end of the day for some important discussions. I would then be sitting on tenterhooks, looking at my watch from time to time wishing that he must leave soon. Conspicuous of my restlessness, he would make a move.

But on one particular occasion, we were involved in a serious discussion over a new project, unmindful of the passing time. Since I had kept the cell phone in a silent mode, I did not take the call from Shanthi. She had given me five missed calls. As I was about to leave the office, I remembered that I had to take Shanthi to the hospital for a check up ; for she was now in her Seventh month of pregnancy.

It was 7.00 p.m when I reached home and the appointment to meet the doctor was at 7.30 p.m. As soon as I entered the house, I apologised to her for being late. She was silent and did not respond to me. As usual, she was angry with me for being late and also not answering the phone. She continued cooking dinner without paying any attention to me. I then asked her to stop cooking and accompany me to the doctor immediately since we had to be there by 7.30 p.m. Further, I also told her that we could have dinner outside. However, Shanthi never responded and continued her work, as though I never existed.

Finally, losing my patience I asked her if we were going to the hospital or not. She then turned back and started to explode, "No ! I am not coming out anywhere today. And by the way, why are you making a great fuss over me today ? After all, I am an unpaid servant maid to you ; one who cooks, cleans and washes everything and who is available 24 × 7 days to you. Why the hell bother about me at all ?"

I tried to pacify her by telling that after meeting the doctor, I planned to buy her a saree she had been requesting me for long. But she was unrelenting and at last, I had to change the date of appointment.

One evening Shanthi's parents came home to have a discussion with me regarding "Vadai Kappu", a small function, celebrating the Eighth month of pregnancy. It was customary that the delivery expenses for the first child was to be borne by the girl's parents. So, immediately after the function was over, Shanthi's mother requested me to send Shanthi along with them and I readily agreed.

Before leaving, Shanthi gave me a long lecture on how I should conduct myself during her absence. Since she was not staying with me, I was not suppose to take any advantage of this. I had to be at home as usual by 6.00 p.m. She also threatened me that she would call me everyday in the evening around 6.00 p.m in the landline. Also, I was to visit her during the weekends without fail. Finally, since I knew cooking, I had to cook my own food and not eat outside. I agreed to abide by all her conditions.

One Friday evening, a colleague, who was a close friend of mine requested me to accompany him for purchasing a LCD television. Since, my boss was on leave, I agreed to go with him and we left the office a little early. After purchasng the LCD TV, I went to his house and assisted him in fixing it on the wall. I joined in the excitement of his children who jumped in great joy over their new LCD television. As I started to leave, the whole family came running after me and entreated me to have dinner with them. Taken away by their kindness, I obliged.

In this chaos, I had left my cell phone in the office itself and hence could not contact Shanthi. As I was returning home, I geared up myself for a good dressing down from her. It was 9.00 p.m when I reached home. As I was fumbling for my keys in my pant pocket, I saw my neighbour, an old and stout lady in her Sixties wobbling up in my direction ; holding a walking stick for support.

Whenever Shanthi was free, she would while away her time with this old woman. What surprised me was the fact that this old lady never left her house at any cost. I would often see her tied to her easy chair; either watching television or gossiping. I was rather shocked as to why this old lady was coming towards me and that too at this odd hour.

I met her mid-way and she stopped suddenly on seeing me. She was huffing and puffing. And finally when her breathing eased, she said that she was feeling bored without Shanthi. She then enquired about Shanthi's health and when her due date was. After I answered all her queries, she smiled at me and wished me all the luck. And before leaving, she asked me why I had come home so late. As I explained everything to her, she listened patiently to me. Finally, she wished to know if I had had my dinner or not and I told her that I had taken it in my friend's house itself. She then turned to leave swiftly after wishing me good night.

I freshened myself and was about to call Shanthi when the phone rang. As soon as I lifted the phone, Shanthi started berating me. She was screaming like hell and I had to hold the receiver a little away from my ears so as not to affect my ear drums. "Why did you return home so late today ?" She began. Before I could offer any explanation to her, she continued, "does your friend not know how to buy a LCD television. Is he a child and should you show him the way ? And why did you have dinner in his house ? I have been trying to contact you from 6.00 p.m and you never even cared to keep me informed about your whereabouts ?"

She continued to rave for a long time and my attempts to interrupt her and tell her that I had left the cell phone in my office did not meet with fruition. After bawling out at me, she abruptly disconnected the call by placing the receiver on the craddle with a loud thud.

Since I was feeling very tired, I did not try to call her again for I knew she was already in a bad temper and I did not like to disturb her. I went to sleep wishing that Shanthi should forgive me and that she should not continue to blast me again over this issue the next day. Just as I was about to close my eyes, I was suddenly overcome with a fit of laughter. Shanthi had set up the old woman to keep a tag on me and pass on the information to her. Hence the old woman was acting like a spy and how stupid and naive of me to have fallen into their trap very easily.

It was 5 a.m. in the morning, when I received another call from Shanthi's house. This time it was from her father. He told me that the labour pains had begun and they were taking Shanthi to the hospital. I got ready quickly and rushed to the hospital. Within two hours, I was blessed with a lovely daughter. It was Shanthi's desire that we name the baby Shruthi. Shruthi was a cute baby and I called her my little princess.

I had been all the while thinking that with the birth of a child, Shanthi would become a little subdued and give up her nagging attitude. But I had guessed wrong. Ofcourse, during the initial period, when she was recouping from childbirth, she remained calm. Infact, she was celebrating her motherhood and kept herself busy fussing over the new born baby. But after a few months, she came back to her old self.

Now, she gave vent to her anger through my daughter. She would either let the baby cry for long by not feeding her or would not change her soiled clothes despite being aware that it was soaked in urine or would avoid giving her a bath. At such times, I would intervene and do the job on her behalf without showing my vexation.

As Shruthi started growing up, she developed a great bond of love and friendship with me. I realised that a man's life is not complete until he receives pure and unblemished love from his offsprings. Slowly, I found myself spending more and more time with my little princess. I accepted Shanthi for whatever she was and adapted to my new life as a henpecked husband. I simply adhered to the adage, if you cannot change the other person, try to change yourself.

It was after the birth of my daughter, that my life turned for good. Very soon, I got promoted as Manager. Though I was given a posh office accommodation, I had to decline the offer for Shanthi was not interested in staying in a flat. She preferred an independent house however small it was to enjoy some privacy in life. With my promotion to the Manager cadre, my responsibilities mounted. I had about ten people reporting to me. One of them was Sneha, a young girl who was newly married. Sneha valued her job so much. She never encouraged piling of papers on her table and would finish any job that I gave her in a jiffy and ask me for more work.

It was the time of auditing and my presence in the office beyond working hours was required. However, fearing that Shanthi would not permit me to work late hours, I planned my work schedule in such a manner so as to be available to the auditors any time during the day and delegated the responsibilities to Sneha to assist them after office hours and she readily agreed without any grumbling.

My boss had many a time requested me to be available to the auditors anytime and I would assure him that I shall take care of everything. Since the things were going on smoothly, he did not question me about my absence in the evenings. In fact, Sneha was carrying out her job so efficiently and saw to it that no problems cropped up.

One Sunday morning, my daughter and I were watching TV when the door bell rang. Shruthi jumped out of my lap and ran to see who it was. I followed her; curious to know who had turned up so early in the morning. I was surprised to see Sneha standing there with a file in her hand. On seeing me she flashed a smile and informed me that the auditors had raised several queries and since they were winding up on Monday, boss had requested her to prepare a draft reply in consultation with me. Knowing very well that I would not come to office on a Sunday, and the work being of a pressing nature, she had come to my house to draft a reply to the audit queries. I asked her to come in. I then introduced her to Shanthi and requested her to get some coffee for her. All of a sudden, Shanthi became morose and her face drained of colour. Without as much as offering a smile to her, she turned to leave in a huff.

It took me almost an hour to clear her doubts and all the while, I kept looking askance to see if Shanthi was bringing the coffee that I had requested. She never did. I went into the kitchen to see if it was ready, but Shanthi was missing. I then prepared some coffee myself and handed it over to Sneha. After seeing her off, I entered the bed room. I saw Shanthi lying on the bed, seething with anger.

I wanted to ask her why she did not bring the coffee. But in order to avoid her snubbing, I just told her that I was famished and asked her why she was not preparing breakfast. Immediately, she got up from the bed and came to me in a fighting spirit. Her eyes were red in anger and her whole body was trembling as she spoke. "How dare you ask that lady to come into my house ?" She blasted. "You must be having really great guts to tell me to make coffee for her. Am I your servant maid to do whatever you say ; that too for some idiotic lady. Just because I am an housewife, are you trying to humiliate me in front of her ?" She screamed at me nonstop. My daughter cowered in fear on hearing her outburst and ran away from there. She sat in the sofa, silently watching the television and turning back from time to time to see if her mother was done with her shouting spell.

I tried my best to explain to her that if Sneha had not taken the pains to come home, a need would have arised for me to go to the office which option also she would not have approved. But she hardly paid any attention to my justification and continued yelling, "can't she hold her doubts for one more day ? Afterall, you spend most of your time in the office and come home very tired. The rest of the evening too, you answer your phone calls and keep yourself busy. It is only on holidays that I am able to pass some time with you and does she have to come trailing behind you even during such times and upset my weekend mood. Am I not entitled to enjoy some privacy with my husband ? In fact you are the culprit. You should have not entertained her. You have time for everyone in this world but me."

That day, after bawling out at me, she entered the kitchen to attend to her work. Though I was rather cut up with Shanthi's rude behaviour I tried to compromise with her later during the day. However, she was not ready for it and continued to sulk. Seeing that her mother was in a bad mood, my daughter lingered around me the whole day and kept away from her mother lest she gets beaten. I appreciated my daughter for her smartness in tackling her mother and saving her skin. Whenever she found her screaming at me, she quietly walked away from the scene of fight. At such times I would remember my own childhood when I felt so aggrieved to see my parents quarrel.

On Monday morning, I was just getting ready for office and saw that Shanthi had still not commenced her cooking. As I was wondering whether to ask her about this or not, my daughter ran to me and said that her mother was not feeling well and hence asked me to eat in the office canteen. I knew that it was a lie and that Shanthi was doing this on purpose. I thanked my little daughter for the information by lifting her up and planting a kiss on her cheek. The poor girl enjoyed being a mouthpiece for her mother and carrying messages for me when we were not talking to each other.

Later, I popped my head into the bedroom and informed her that I was leaving for office but Shanthi did not stir. She continued to lie down, not caring to give me a send off at the door step, which was her usual practice.

Immediately, after having my breakfast in the canteen, I went around looking for Sneha. She was always very punctual and would be in her seat by sharp 9.00 a.m She would never be late without taking prior permission from me. It was already 10.00 a.m and when Sneha had still not turned up, I started getting anxious as to what could be delaying her. For all the important audit papers were under her custody and I had to submit a report to the boss.

As time kept passing by, I started getting restless. However, presuming that it should be something important that was holding her, I decided not to disturb her. I went to the boss and briefed him about my predicament and aplogised to him. Further, I requested him to give me some more time to submit the audit reply.

It was 2.00 p.m. when I entered my room after having my lunch. I was rather surprised to see Sneha sitting in my room. She was not her usual self and as I looked at her, I realised that she had been crying. She was so depressed and on seeing me, she stood up and amidst tears explained to me the cause for coming so late to office. I was appalled to hear her sad story.

Just after I left the house, Shanthi had somehow managed to obtain the address of Sneha from my office and had gone to her house. Sneha was just about to start to office along with her husband when Shanthi barged into their house and bawled out at her. She told her that she did not want her to come to her house again ; however headgoing the matter might be and nor was she suppose to phone to me for any clarifications after office hours as she despised it very much. Further, she blamed her that she had been responsible for a big fight that ensued after she left the house.

A small crowd had gathered in front of Sneha's house on hearing her loud screams. In order to evoke their pity, Shanthi spoke disparagingly of Sneha's attitude thus creating bad vibes in the minds of the onlookers.

Since Sneha's husband happened to be a timid guy, he did not combat with her. Instead he placated her anger by promising her that this won't happen again and sent her away. However, embarrassed by the derogatory words spoken by Shanthi, he advised Sneha that, if there was any possibility of obtaining a transfer, she could try for the same immediately for it was always safe to keep away from trouble.

And now Sneha was sitting in front of me pleading that I somehow talk it out with boss and get her a transfer to a different location. I readily agreed to help her out. For I was sure that Shanthi would not let her live in peace. She was sure to keep a tag on her by setting up spies all around and make her life miserable.

That night when I reached home, Shanthi came to me with a cup of coffee and asked me if Sneha had come to the office. I really felt ashamed of her debase behaviour towards Sneha. Though I was boiling inside with anger I did not show it to her. Maintaining my cool, I told her about Sneha's request for transfer to a different branch. Immediately she heaved a sigh of relief.

I silently bore all the torments that Shanthi was inflicting on me day after day without retaliating. For I had by now got used to her unpredictable character and had learnt how to tackle the same. But it was my daughter Shruthi for whom I felt great sympathy and started to worry a lot about her. For whenever she found her mother hysterically screaming at me, she cringed in fear. Immediately, she would come running and cling to me. Enraged by this, Shanthi would start hitting the poor girl mercilessly for no fault of hers. This really provoked me and was getting on my nerves. After all, I am a human being too and for how long could I tolerate the atrocities committed by her ? One fine day, I found myself losing control on my emotions.

I acted on impulse and it has resulted in my separation from my loving daughter, for which malicious act, I keep repenting each and every day.

I just returned from office one evening, when I observed that Shanthi was in low spirits. Even before I asked her about it, she came to me with a sad face and informed me that her sister was admitted in the hospital due to Leptospyrosis. Since Shruthi was having her vacation, I told her that if she desired she could go and stay with her sister in the hospital till she recovers. Shanthi was excited to hear this and on the next day itself, she went to her house and after leaving Shruthi with her grandmother, headed to the hospital. She stayed in the hospital for almost a week and on Sunday morning, she phoned up and informed me that her sister was going to be discharged and asked me to pick her up in the afternoon.

On reaching the hospital, I found that Shanthi was busy in packing up the things to leave while my Sister-in-Law was in deep slumber. Just then, a nurse came in and asked Shanthi to settle the hospital dues and so she accompanied her. Suddenly, my sister-in-law woke up and was rather surprised to see me sitting in the room. I told her that Shanthi had gone to pay the bill and she will be back in a few minutes. She tried to get up but was finding it very difficult ; for her hands were too weak from the numerous shots that she was given. Seeing her struggle, I offered my hand for support. By holding it, she tried to lift herself up. At that point of time, Shanthi entered the room. Seeing me holding her sister's hand, she became furious at me. Immediately, she lunged forward and shoving me aside, helped her sister prop up on a pillow.

After the discharge formalities were completed, I booked a call taxi and sent them home. I then followed them in my bike. On reaching my mother-in-law's house, I had dinner and returned home along with my daughter. I noticed that Shanthi was in one of her bad moods and was avoiding me. She did not speak to me nor did she reply to any of my questions..

It was around 9.00 p.m. when we reached home. I was feeling very tired and looked forward to a good sleep. As I parked my bike and came walking, I saw Shanthi standing at the doorstep with a scowling face. She was blocking my way and hence I could not get in. As I approached her, she started firing at me, "I never knew that you were a good opportunist. Seeing that no one was around, you coolly thought of exploiting my sister, isn't it ?"

Seeing that her mother was about to start a conflict with me, Shruthi dashed out of the hall and clung to me. Dumbfounded by her grating words I said, "I don't understand what you are talking about !"

"Don't pretend to be very innocent. You owe me an explanation as to why you touched my sister ?" she snapped.

Confused as to why she was condemning me, I asked, "is it wrong to give a helping hand to a needy person ? Seeing her futile attempts in trying to get up from the bed, I thought of assisting her and there ends the matter."

"Oh is it ? Is my sister an old granny ? Can't she help herself to get up. She is a young girl and after several attempts, she should have eventually succeeded. Who the hell are you to help her ? I am sure your intention was not to help her but to touch her. Since there was no one around, you wished to take advantage of the situation in a selfish manner !"

Her derogatory words were jarring to my ears. I was fatigued and was longing to have a sleep. I was in no mood for an argument and asked her to take her hand off from the door and let me go in. But the sharp words that came from her jolted me. Not allowing me to step in she blared, "you have not answered my question yet as to why you touched my sister. This shows how mean you are. Am I not enough for you ? Do you plan to keep my sister by your side too ?"

I at once realised that God was testing my patience. I could not tolerate her nasty words that she was caviling at me. Immediately, stung by her sharp words, I slapped her across her face and asked her to shut up.

Infuriated by this, Shanthi came out and dragged Shruthi away from me. Shruthi was sad that her parents were at loggerheads. However, she wanted to take side with me. Immediately, she pleaded with me that I lift her up and did not like to accompany her mother.

Provoked by her disobedience, Shanthi started beating her black and blue. Pulling her inside forcibly, she kept telling her, "your father has never before hit me like this. He must have become mad and it is better if you keep away from him."

But Shruthi was in no mood to listen to her. She squatted on the floor and started crying aloud, looking at me pitifully ; expecting me to intervene and help her out from this situation.

But I stood outside, utterly abashed over my brutal action. I wondered why I was not able to control my emotions and adhere to the resolution of not losing my temper.

Shruthi kept crying aloud and calling me inside. Furious over this, Shanthi started kicking the poor girl mercilessly with her leg, right in front of my eyes. Unable to bear the beatings, the little girl sprawled to the floor.

I once again made an attempt to enter inside to save my daughter from the wrath of my wife, but Shanthi was steadfast in her decision in not letting me in and she said, "this is my house and since you have become daring enough to hit me, you have no place here henceforth. Go and find yourself a place in some Orphanage." With these words, she slammed the door behind me with a loud bang.

I silently sat down on the portico dwelling at length about the sudden turn of events. Why was Shanthi so incorrigible and suspecting me for each and everything? It was a great pity to see my little princess beaten up by her for no fault of hers. I just could not tolerate this and the fact that I could not protect her as a father was still more painful to my heart.

For the first time since marriage, an odd feeling crossed my mind. Nothing that I ever do would please Shanthi. She would always keep carping at me for one thing or the other. Probably she was taking too much advantage of my lenient nature. I had to punish her for taking me for granted. I decided to leave her !

Perhaps, if I left the family, apart from teaching Shanthi a lesson for her arrogant behaviour, I would also concomitantly be saving my daughter from getting beaten constantly on account of me. For Shanthi was often giving vent to her anger over me by hitting the poor girl.

I sat there glumly in the dark ; weighing the pros and cons of my drastic decision of leaving the family. My conscious was pricking me and was against my taking a decision, especially when I was angry.

Trying to make peace with her for one last time, I stood up and kept pacing the veranda up and down, in an insane manner. I saw that the bedroom window was partly open. I went and peeped through it. Shruthi was in sound sleep, cuddled to her mother. Not wanting to disturb her, I called out Shanthi's name in a hushed tone. Shanthi did not stir. I could not make out whether she was really fast asleep or was just pretending. I came back to the portico and sat down.

Once again, my mind started revolving on the thoughts of leaving the family. Seeing my daughter snuggled close to her mother, I thought perhaps if I left the family, Shanthi would take loving care of my daughter. Now I was even more determined to leave. For the good of my daughter !.

Over come with fatigue, I lay down on the chill floor with my hands behind my head, contemplating on whether the decision I was about to take was the right thing or not. It was December and the night was very cold and a cool wind kept blowing. Still not sure about my decision and indulging in vain thoughts as to how I should go about with my life, I slowly drifted away into sleep.

It was 5 O clock early in the morning, when I was woken up by the chirping noises of the birds all around.

Shanthi did not come out looking for me, nor did she bother to give me dinner. She uncaringly let me sleep on the chill floor. She was so heartless and I was sure that even if I was gone, she would hardly feel the loss. She was a die-hard woman.

A cool breeze was blowing sending shivers across me. I looked up at the bright shining moon and the twinkling stars. The trees swaying in the wind and the chattering of the birds all around soothed my rather turbulent mind. I admired these forces of nature which existed independently on their own. Silently they went about their activities enjoying themselves, without any expectations. It was we human beings who long for a company and suffer as a result of that bond.

Suddenly, my mind was crystal clear. I too decided to lead an independent life bereft of any attachments. I longed for freedom without any ties. After making up my mind, I stood up and slowly started moving on.

Filled with a pang of remorse at having to part with my daughter, I turned back for one last time and tearfully bid good bye to the house. Strong emotional forces were resisting my action. Trying hard to suppress them, I said to myself, "No Turning Back" and continued to walk.

If my daughter was to lead a happy life, I had to leave. Then, she would be able to grow-up in a peaceful atmosphere without parent rivalry and also be spared of the beatings. For the good of my loving daughter, I had to leave ! I walked in the direction that my legs took me, until I reached Koyambedu bus stand.

Just at that moment, I saw a bus about to leave for Kanchipuram. Immediately I got into it and left Chennai with a heavy heart.

It was 11.00 p.m. already and Ramanathan was feeling rather drowsy. Stifling a yawn, he said, "it is really sad to know that Shanthi was rude to you and had ill-treated you so much ; for I know her as a kind and timid girl. Stop worrying this second. I promise to help you wholeheartedly."

Drawing his brows together in confusion, Ramanathan continued, "by the way what beats me is the fact that you are working as a priest in a temple. You could have found a good job here and rented a large house instead of staying in this dungeon."

Ramanathan saw a smile quiver on his lips as he began, "Ah..... that is a funny story indeed ! I was neither sure nor had any idea as to how to go about with my life. I believed that my visit to the temples would help me in clearing all my confusions and give me some peace. I wished to receive God's blessings and pray to Him to show me the right path.

First, I went to Kachapaeshwarar Temple. After coming round the temple several times, I sat down in front of the Vinayaga Statue at the entrance of the temple. I was really fatigued and hungry. I was prepared to face any kind of hardship in life, but never wished to return home. I closed my eyes and sat in deep meditation. As I did this, I told myself that the first person who passed my way as soon as I opened my eyes will be the one from whom I would seek help.

To my dismay, an old man who was the pujari of the main temple, from whom I had received prasad a few minutes ago was crossing me. He was returning home and I suddenly realised that I had been sitting there for long, engrossed in my ardent prayers ; unmindful of the passing time. I trailed behind the old man calling out to him.

When at last he came to a halt, I went up to him and requested him to inform me about any cheap accommodation that was available nearby. The old man gave me a cursory glance from head to toe. Before he could shower me with questions, I briefed him about my background. I told him that I was a B.Com graduate and since I had lost both my parents in childhood I grew up in my aunt's house. Not wanting to be a burden to my aunt anymore, I have come down to Kanchipuram in connection with a job. I also lied to him that I was a bachelor and a single room accommodation would be more than sufficient to me.

Impressed with the details I had given, the old man volunteered that he had an outhouse which was vacant and invited me to have a look at the same. If I was interested, he was willing to rent it out to me. Happy that my first attempt met with success, I accompanied the old man to his house.

I cleaned up the small room and started to live there. The first two days, I spent the mornings by visiting the temples in Kanchipuram. I then went to a hotel, had my fill and returned to my room and slept. The old Pujari was skeptcial about my lingering in the house the whole day and on the third day, before leaving to the temple, he stopped by and enquired as to why I was not going out for work.

I then told him that, I am yet to find a job and was confident of finding one very soon. Then just by fluke I added, if there is any one you are aware of who could offer me a job as Accountant, please let me know. On hearing this, the old man let out a guffaw. And he said, "who do I know ? All I know is the Lord. He takes care of all my needs and I shall put forth your request to

Him." With these words, he rushed out to attend to his chores.

To my astonishment, he came to my room once again that night with a smile writ large on his face and said, "see how courteous is God. He has answered my prayers immediately. Our temple management committee is looking for an Accountant and when I apprised them about you, the Trustee wished to see you." I joined as an Accountant and spent most of my time in the temple.

The old man had a fascination for me and was bent upon helping me out. For, after a month, he once again came to me and in a hushed tone, said, "I know that the amount of Rs. 2000 you received this month as salary would not be sufficient to meet all your needs. I have got some good news for you. The priest who performs the puja for Lord Vinayaga is leaving for better prospects. I advice you to take up that job too. Apart from a monthly salary of Rs.1500, all the money that people drop in the Aarathi plate would belong to you. Everyday, you are sure to get a collection of around three hundred rupees. And on festive occasions, you could receive more than a thousand rupees."

Working as a priest was not my cup of tea. I was not interested in whatever the old man was blabbering, but knowing that he would not like to be interrupted, I listened to him patientily and finally when he was done, I voiced my opinion to him.

I told him point blank that I was not the fitting person for that job and that I did not know the procedure of performing Vinayaga puja. Upset over my reply he said rather curtly, "I shall give you the required training for doing the puja. Come with me tomorrow morning."

He did not give me a choice and I did not wish to disappoint the old man. I decided to obey him implicitly. On the next day, he handed over a small book and asked me to by-heart the slokas which he had marked in it. After a week's training, I became confident of perfoming the puja all alone. The long hair and the red vermillion mark on my forehead are the suggestions of the old man. At first, I was really embarrassed to come to the temple without a shirt. Eventually, I got used to this dress code."

Swaminathan laughed as he finished his story and added, "well, I know it is one of the foolish decisions I had ever taken in my life. However, I don't have any regrets over that. I am happy and enjoy doing my work. I am still perplexed about the old man who had taken all out efforts in seeing to my comforts. He had got his only daughter married away a few years back and is living with his wife.

From time to time I carry out errands for them and now he keeps coaxing me to get married and settle in life. I don't know how he would take it if I tell him that I have a grown up daughter. The only worry I have now is my daughter. I left her when she was in fourth standard. I am sure she must have completed her tenth standard now. I pray for her everyday. I long to see her ...." Swaminathan broke off at this point and he became speechless.

It was nearing midnight and Ramanathan stood up stifling another yawn. "I know you must be missing your daughter a lot. I promise to unite you with your family very soon. Tomorrow, I shall meet Shanthi and tell her about our meeting. On Thursday morning, I shall bring Shanthi and your daughter here and so be ready to accompany them back home."

Swaminathan had been praying God every day to bring about a union with his daughter. He had faith in God and was waiting patiently for that auspicious moment. And when at last the moment arrived, he could not believe himself. He pinched himself serveral times to verify if he was having a good dream or was it a reality.

However, Swaminathan had his own doubts. He was not sure if Shanthi would accept him back into her life. He had ditched her once and what if she had not forgiven him yet. Now Ramanathan was willing to act as a go between in uniting them after six long years.

While he was happy at the prospect of meeting his daughter, he feared about the outcome of their meeting. He never wished that Ramanathan should face the brunt of Shanthi's anger on account of him and so hesitantly, he said, "though you know Shanthi very well even before me, I don't know if she will be kind to you If you discuss about me. I don't like her to behave in an arrogant manner and insult you unnecessarily."

Ramanathan cut in, "you leave that to me ! I have a knack of getting on with people. I have compromisied the fights of brothers who had been bitter enemies and brought about the union of couples who were opting for divorce. I always compare myself with the green grass which never gets crushed when people walk over it nor does it hurt them. Just like the grass, I don't get crushed when people burden me with their problems and while solving them, if I have to face any criticism, I swallow the bitter pill silently and don't take it to heart. I have learnt to take it in my stride."

Valli's heart skipped several beats, when she heard the foot steps. She was sitting inside her small hut, built in the premises of construction of a new flat in Kodambakkam. She knew that her husband was back, fully drunk.

Just a while ago, Velan had left the hut in great anger. He had come in to have his lunch. After having his lunch, he lay down for some rest. Just then, his six month year old son started to cry and Valli lifted him from the craddle. After nursing him, she put him back into the craddle and rocked him to sleep.

Velan was in a mood for a bout of sex that afternoon and hence he called out to her. Valli at once knew his intention but she was not willing to comply with his request as she had plenty of chores to be done. Telling him to wait until it was night, she cooly walked out. When it came to sex, Velan would never take a no for an answer.

Annoyed by her refusal, Velan asked, "howcome you have become so daring enough these days ?"

"Come here immediately !" He ordered his wife.

But Valli did not bother and continued with her work. Her lackadaisical attitude provoked him and he shouted, "did you not hear me ?"

Nonchalantly Valli repeated, "I told you to wait until it is night !"

"You have started dictating terms to me ? Have you forgotten the hardship I underwent in order to wed you ? It is not for nothing that I lifted the two huge rocks and got married to you ? And now you are ill-treating me by denying me my pleasure ?" He screamed at her.

Valli was fed up of hearing this discourse. Whenever

a quarrel broke out between them, Velan always referred to this incident.

Both Velan and Valli belong to a village near Salem in Tamilnadu. Since the income out of agriculture was fast dwindling, Velan decided to look for fresh pastures. Velan had heard that many individual house owners were dismantling their houses and selling it to the flat promoters and Velan felt that Chennai was the best place to flourish. Through an acquaintance of his, he got a job as coolie in Chennai and moved down here with his wife and six months old son to eke out his living.

This village from which they hail from followed a unique practice. Before giving away the girl in marriage to a man, the members belonging to both the families gather together at the market place, where one can find enormous rocks weighing 60 kg and 90 kg respectively. The bridgroom has to lift up each of these rocks one by one to prove his strength to everyone. They believe that by lifting up the heavy rocks, the man is strong enough and is capable of shouldering any kind of hardship in life.

Those unable to lift the rocks will have to pay a fine of rupees three hundred to the Village Head who uses it for buying betel leaves for old women and choclates for the children. Earlier in the bygone days, men were strong enough and they lifted a single rock weighting 150 kg which eventually got divided into two rocks in the modern times. But even after this, young men are finding it difficult to lift the rocks and opt to pay the fine.

On seeing Valli, Velan was much enamored by her beauty. In order to prove how much he loved her, he tried to exhibit his strength. After several attempts, he finally succeeded in lifting the huge rocks one after another, amidst great cheers and applause.

Everyone congratulated Valli and told her that she was lucky to be blessed with a strong man as her husband. Valli felt proud and stood there blushing. However, it was only after her marriage, that she got to know about his true colours. For Velan was a sex maniac and he tormented her day in and day out. Many a time, Valli had pathetically complained about his rough handling of her but he would silence her with the words, "it is not for nothing that I had lifted the huge rocks !" Slowly, she resigned to her fate and bore it all silently.

Her mother had reassured her time and again that the birth of a child would transform him. For the child would draw the father's attention thus keeping him away from her. But even that, she realised proved false in her case. For instead of falling in love with his son, he was engulfed with a feeling of jealousy as Valli was now spending much of her time with her son. Of late, she started denying him his sexual pleasures using her son as a pretext and this was getting on his nerves.

Infuriated over her denial, he yelled, "if you don't come here within a minute, you had it from me today!" But Valli did not budge. She hardly seemed to care for his threat. Swearing at her, Velan stood up and left the place seething with anger.

Suddenly Valli was gripped with fear. She was sure that he must have gone to have a drink. Usually, Valli would run behind him and pull him back ; for when he was drunk, he would behave in a very violent manner and she would end up with bruises all over her body.

But today, he had walked out swiftly not giving her a chance to stop him.

And now that her husband had returned, Valli was filled with panic and was scared out of her wits. After bolting the door behind him, Velan came and sat down beside her. Valli was breast feeling her son. Silently, without caring for him.

"Are you nursing the baby ?" He asked with a wicked smile on his face.

Valli did not reply and nervously kept staring at his face.

"Well, continue you job !" He said sliding his hand inside her blouse.

The look on his face frightened her and she at once knew that he was upto something sinister. As Velan started mauling her breast, tears sprang from her eyes. However, Valli decided not to object for she was afraid that he might hit her mercilessly. He then moved on to her nipple and began tugging at it. Ruthlessly, he started twitching it. With tears streaming down her face, Valli sat there quietly without resisting. Suddenly, he started squeezing it savagely not minding the milk that was dribbling over his fingers. The pain he was inducing caused her to squirm. This did not however move him nor did it stop him from tormenting her. He was fully bent on taking out his revenge for her non-compliance.

Realising that he was in no way going to stop his torture, Valli begged him through her sobs, "please stop doing that, it hurts a lot !"

Hardly did he care for her pleas ! Stretching it even further, he said, "shut up your dirty mouth. You need to be taught a lesson for disbedience !"

"Nowadays your son comes first and you even started disrespecting me, isn't it ?" He shouted, inflicting more pain than ever. Valli could not endure it any longer and started writhing in excruciating pain.

The tears were by now forming rivers on her face and Valli started whimpering. It was only after agonizing her for a few more minutes ; which seemed like eternity to her, that he softened a little and decided to stop his brutal act. Yanking her nipple one last time, he ordered, "put the baby in the craddle and come here !" Wiping away her tears, Valli stood up. After rocking the baby to sleep, she obliged him.

When they were in the midst of love making, her son woke up and started to cry. Once again, Velan's anger grew up by leaps and bounds. Valli made an effort to get up, but Velan pulled her back. He got up swiftly and walked to the craddle, cursing the baby under his breath. "It is after your coming that my wife has lost her love for me !" He said as he rocked the craddle forcibly. His son now started to scream even louder and Valli could not bear this and it was heart rending to her. "Close your eyes and sleep now, you stupid fellow", he yelled, rocking the craddle back and forth, in a mad frenzy. The craddle rose so high and hit the wall with a loud thud. The next moment the cries of the baby came to a standstill. Thinking the baby had fallen asleep, Velan returned to his wife.

After a few minutes, when Valli came to see her son, she was in for a shock. There was a huge bump on his forehead and blood was oozing out from it. Lifting up her son from the craddle, Valli ran out crying for help. The workers who had gone out for lunch had just returned. One of the older men, felt the pulse of the baby and informed her that the baby was already dead.

Valli let out an ear shattering scream. She then started rolling on the ground crying her heart out. She was bawling out at her husband that he was the cause of her son's death. A small crowd had gathered around Valli and the women folk were pacifying her. Her rantings continued for long but it did very little good in bringing back her son's life. Some one in the neighbourhood stealthily informed the police about the happenings here. As Valli kept berating her husband for his selfish attitude, she saw two policemen coming towards her.

Velan was at once taken to task. He was handcuffed and taken away in a jeep. Valli sat there bewildered, not sure of her next step to be taken now. On the one hand, she lost her beloved son, who just started to smile back at her and on the other, her husband was being taken away for imprisonment on the charges of murder.

Shanthi, who was then five years old was playing in the sand, building temples. On seeing the policemen, she became frightened and started running back to her house, which was just opposite to the construction site. She kept on prattling to her mother about the happenings on the site. Parvathi was then having her lunch and on hearing her daughter babble, she gobbled up her food and came out to find the reason for her daughter's alarm. She saw that all the workers had abandoned their work and gathered together. They were talking in hushed tones and Parvathi could not understand what exactly was the issue. When she heard a long piercing cry arise from the group, she became rather curious and started walking towards them, with Shanthi trailing behind her. One of the women informed her about the pathetic event that had occurred some time back. On learning about Valli's sorrowful plight, Parvathi was at once filled with empathy for her.

Eversince the construction of a flat opposite to her house began, Parvathi was finding it very difficult to control her daughter. Shanthi would often run away to the site to watch the various activities going on there. However, there was one good thing that Parvathi was glad about. Her feeding ritual, which was an arduous task now became a simple one. All Parvathi had to do was to step out of her house with the plate. Watching the work going on there, Shanthi would swallow up everything that she stuffed into her mouth without making a fuss. On seeing Parvathi standing outside, Valli would come for having a small talk with her. She would linger around, until Parvathi was done with her chore of feeding her daughter. Slowly, Valli became close to her.

Valli sat there wailing with her dead son on her lap. One of the women workers was packing up Valli's things. She was getting ready to accompany her to the village to perform the last rites of the child. On seeing Valli in this piteous state, Parvathy's heart melted and she started comforting her. After pacifying Valli, Parvathi went back to her house to get some money. Handing it over to Valli, she asked her to leave immediately. As Valli left the place with the corpse of her dead son, Parvathi was moved to tears.

After the funeral ceremony was over, Valli continued to live with her parents. During her stay, Valli noticed the difficulties her father was facing in order to make both ends meet. Her family was a large one and three of her younger sisters were yet to be married. Valli realised that it was not right on her part to continue staying there and be an additional burden to her father. Instead, she decided to go out for work and support the family. She was confident that the building contractor would offer her some job or the other. After convincing her father suitably, she returned to Chennai. She spent her money in a thrifty manner and once in a while went to the village and handed over her savings to her father.

But after an year, Valli once again found herself at the cross-roads. The construction of the building was over and the contractor asked her to go back to her village ; promising that he would call her again when he commenced his new project, a few months later. After packing up her things, Valli was walking towards the busstand, when all of a sudden she saw Shanthi playing outside her house. Parvathi was calling out to her to have her food. Valli stopped by to say good bye to them. Valli then explained her predicament and requested her if she was aware of anyone in the neighbourhood who could offer her a job. Further, she vouched that she was willing to do any kind of job that was given to her and all that she required was a little food and some space to sleep.

Suddenly, a thought crossed Parvathi's mind. She was then carrying her second daughter and was in her last leg of pregnancy. She was in dire need of some domestic help as she was unable to cope with all the household work. She had herself been in the look out for someone who could assist her. She wished to help Valli by offering her a job and keeping her in the house. Immediately, she phoned up to her husband to seek his opinion on this.

Her husband was however against this. He warned her that she was buying trouble. He explained to her that it was not proper to keep a lady at home ; that too, someone whose husband was in jail. This could lead to many unforseen problems in the future and so he gave a negative reply to this. But Parvathi was steadfast in her decision and she started pleading with him that it was her responsibility and she would see to it that no problems cropped up on account of her. She further justified to him that, Valli was an innocent and soft lady and her staying with them would cause no harm to anybody. Finally, her husband relented by admonishing her that if any untoward events turned up due to this, it was up to her to tackle it and he would stay out of it.

The entry of Valli was a turning point in Parvathi's life. Valli took care of all the household jobs and never let Parvathi do any work. Parvathi now had plenty of time on her hand. She whiled away her leisure time by watching serials in the television.

After completing her job, Valli would also sit and watch the serials along with Parvathi. At times, Valli would lament the loss of her son or narrate stories of her childhood. But what topped her conversation always was the horrific life that she had led with her husband. She would recount to her without any inhibitions, the sexual tortures she had undergone with her husband. Parvathi would become so much engrossed with her tales and listen to them with rapt attention.

Parvathi's life infact was no different from that of Valli. She had also faced many hardships with her husband initially. To her husband, sex was the essence of life and the be all and the end all of life. But Parvathi completely differed from his views. To her it was just a means of procreation. Their fights often narrowed down to the topic of sex.

However, Parvathi never discussed about these fights to anyone including her mother. After a few years when her understanding of her husband got better ; especially after the birth of Shanthi, she learnt to handle her husband in a tactful manner. She slept the whole day with her daughter and kept herself busy after her husband's return from office. After handing over her daughter to him, she would start preparing dinner and keep herself very busy until it was late night. Whenever he expressed his desire for sex, she would immediately give him one reason or the other. She had formulated a set of excuses to give him in order to evade sex when she was in no mood for it. She would complain of a migrane headache, premenstrual cramps, dishes to be washed, clothes to be dried or that she was having her periods. Each time he heard her pretexts, he would leave in great resentment, cursing her under his breath, "you have time for everything in this world ; but when it comes to pleasing me, you neither have time nor energy for that. It is all my fate !" And he would start sulking for the rest of the day. In the beginning, Parvathi used to take his sarcastic comments to heart and suffer from mental agony. In the long run, she overlooked his grouches and learnt to take it in her stride.

After Valli's coming, Parvathy's life turned topsy-turvy. Valli took care of all her works. Now Parvathy was left with ample time. One day, her husband kept flirting around her. When Parvathy did not respond to this, he yelled at her, "these days you have nothing to do. Can't you atleast now satisfy my pleasures ?" Parvathy realised that with a live-in servant-maid, she could no more hoodwink her husband. For she was sure that he would regard her scornfully. Hence she tried to keep her husband pleased in this front.

The fact that now she could not elude him was getting on her nerves. Gradually, after a bout of sex with him, she became irascible and lost her temper for no reason at all. She started quarrelling with him over trifles. And what astonished Parvathi the most was the sudden transformation in her husband's character. Unlike before, he did not take offense of her outbursts. Now that his sexual appetite was being appeased, he did not care about her frequent flare-ups and let her boss over him. He became a henpecked husband.

Shanthi grew up in such an atmosphere ; observing her mother nagging her father the wholeday. She was also surprised by her father's taciturn nature, despite her mother's rudeness. She formed a general opinion in her mind that this was how it was in all the households : women bossed over their husbands everywhere. Shanthi imbibed her mother's trait. Immediately after marriage, she started walking in her mother's foot steps.

Swaminathan thus became a victim of her poor upbringing. Silently, he tolerated her nitpicking nature without retorting. He hoped that Shanthi would soften a little in the due course. But when things were getting too far, he could not take it any longer. He decided that it was high time to retailiate and hence backed away from her life.

However Shanthi did have a soft heart. Only it was embedded deep inside a shell. On that cold night, when she had quarrelled with Swaminathan and locked him out of the house ; without showing him due respect, she knew that she was overdoing it. She at once felt guilty of her overbearing attitude and wished to make it up with him in a short while.

But as luck would have it, her thoughts got diverted when her eyes fell on her daughter. Shruthi was lying on the floor, whimpering in pain. Her face was swollen and there were bruises at different parts of her body. On seeing the battered condition of her daughter, Shanthi's heart went out to her.

As she bent down to inspect the wounds, Shruthi flinched and complained that it hurt a lot. She repented for her shameful act of beating her daughter in a ruthless manner. She then started to pacify her daughter. Applying some soothing gel over the injuries, she justified to her that since she was famished, fatigued and angry with her father, she had given vent to her vexed feelings by beating her black and blue. Further, she assured her that she would not repeat this again.

Shanthi was redressing her violent behaviour by mollycoddling her so much so that Shruthi forgot all about her father. Despite the pain, she was laughing and happily chatting away with her mother. Thus Shruthi had drawn her attention for the rest of the evening.

Knowing that Shanthi would be too tired to cook dinner, her mother had prepared idlies and packed it up for her. After feeding a few idlies to Shruthi, she asked her to go and sleep. It was only now that Shruthi remembered her father. For, it was he who would tell her stories at bedtime and make her sleep. Shruthi wanted to go and call her father in, but immediately changed her mind, lest her mother gets angry with her once again. She wished to be in the good books of her mother ; especially now, when she was being pampered by her. After all, it was because of taking her father's side and clinging to him that had aroused her mother's temper in the first place ; which had resulted in her getting beaten up.

She stood there silently beside her mother not knowing what to do. Finally, she entreated her to accompany her to the bedroom and make her sleep. But Shanthi refused by telling her that she had plenty of jobs to do. Shruthi however persisted that she could carry out her chores after she fell asleep. Usually, Shanthi would not give in to such demands of her daughter and spoil her. But today, she was bent on keeping her daughter happy and so after abandoning all her works, walked towards the bedroom.

On her way, she stopped to open the door and call her husband in. As she reached for the bolt, she hesitated for a moment and then suddenly withdrew her hand. She decided that she should not be the first to compromise. Why did he not knock the door so far? Ofcourse, she had behaved in a rough manner with him. But this was not the first time and she had been rude to him in the past as well. And if he was really cut up with her because of her harsh words, he could have atleast called out his daughter. All along, it had been him who had taken the first step towards compromising. Why change the usual practice ? She did not wish to set a new trend by being the first to compromise. As she moved on, she thought that men had always to be kept under control, no matter what! They should not be let to take an upper hand and boss over them.

Thus, in a resolute manner, she walked to the bedroom and lay down beside her daughter. Nestling close to her, she started telling her stories ; all the while straining her ears for any tapping sound on the door.

It had been a very tiring day for Shanthi. The discharge formalities in the hospital was an arduous task and she had to run from pillar to post in order to get her sister out of the hospital. Shanthi had exerted herself so much so that by evening when she reached home after completing the ordeal successfully, she was fully depleted of energy.

Besides, the argument she had with her husband left her mentally exhausted. As Shruthi attentively listened to the story, she found her mother drifting away to sleep quite often. She had to keep prodding her from time to time to continue with the story.

By the time, she was finished with the story, Shruthi was asleep. Slowly, Shanthi got up from the bed ; careful not to disturb her. As she turned to leave, she found her daughter's hand tugging at her saree, whining that she must not leave her alone. Once again, Shanthi obliged and lay down beside her. As she kept patting her, so as to make her sleep, she was herself overcome by sleep.

Swaminathan was sitting out in the cold night with a turbulant mind over the turn of events that occurred in the evening. He was himself feeling very tired and hungry and he sat there silently, expecting that Shanthi would come out and call him in. It was dinner time and when she had still not bothered to serve him food, he decided to make the first move. He stood up and went to the door step. He rang the bell several times, but there was no any response. He then started banging the door frantically. However his attempts were only futile. For Shanthi was already in deep slumber.

He stood there helplessly not knowing what to do. He then noticed that the bed room window was open a crack and so hurriedly walked in that direction. He shouted out her name many times but Shanthi did not respond even to this. She was lying there like a log of wood ; unware of anything that was happening aound her. When his attempts to wake her up met with failure, he decided to give up. He was very upset over her negligence and lackadaisical attitude.

Hunger made him wild and he found his temper rising. Suddenly he realised that mother and daughter were cuddled close to each other, which was a very unusual thing. It was a feast to his eyes. For, Shruthi always kept away from her mother and remained close to him and she would not sleep without daddy beside her. For once, he was happy to see both of them lying together. Perhaps they had resolved their fight they had in the evening and were in good terms with each other. He reveled in the momentary pleasure.

And once again, his mind reverted to his previous decision of leaving his family. This time, it was on account of his loving daughter. He had to leave them if his daughter was to grow in a happy atmosphere, bereft of parent rivalry which according to him had a bad effect on the growing child. He was confident that his daughter would continue to live in peace and enjoy her mother's undivided attention and love. Probably, when he was not around, there was no reason for Shanthi to either get provoked or lose her temper. In turn, there was no need for her to give vent to her anger on her only target - his daughter. Shanthi's arrogance was going beyond his limit of tolerance and it was high time that he walked out of her life. Without as much as a word to his little princess, he cooly walked out of her life.

Shanthi's eyes glared from the sun's rays which penetrated deep into the room through the window. She observed that it was dawn already and as she looked up at the clock, she was horrorstruck ; for it was 6 O clock. It was her habit that immediately after getting up from bed, she would go to the puja room to obtain the blessings from God for a hassle free day, after which only she would commence her activities of the day. But today, her first thought was about her husband. She felt bad about the ill-treatment she had meted out to him. He must have slept on the cold floor the whole night and that too without having dinner. Evading her usual ritual, she rushed to the door with her heart pounding. But to her dismay, Swaminathan was not there in the portico. She stood there for long wondering where he might have gone.

She then opened the gate and went out to see if he was lingering around with any of the neighbours. Not finding him anywhere in the vicinity, she returned home dejected.

Just then, Shruthi woke up and not finding anyone beside her, started running out fearfully. On seeing her mother, she asked, "where is father ?"

Not answering her, Shanthi commanded, "go have your bath and get ready for school. Your father will come shortly !"

The school was reopening for the second term and it was the usual practice that her father would drop her at school on the first day.

Since her father was not around, Shruthi once again asked her mother, "will he come before I start to school? He had promised to take me to school today."

"Ofcourse, he will come and take you to school." She said and continued to toast a few slices of bread to pack her lunch box ; for she was in no mood to prepare breakfast.

When at last, Shruthi was ready, Shanthi gave her a bowl of chocos mixed in milk and told her to eat quickly.

It was getting late to school and still there was no any sign of Swaminathan. Shanthi decided to take her daughter to school by an auto. Though her mother was accompanying her to school, Shruthi looked rather grumpy. All the while she was thinking of her father, whom she missed a lot and before getting down from the auto, voiced her opinion to her mother. "if only you had not sent him out of the house last night, he would have taken me to school in his motor bike." Assuring her that her father would be at home when she returned from school, Shanthi waved good bye to her.

It was 11 a.m. and Shanthi was enraged over her husband's uncaring attitude. There was no way that she could contact him for he had left his cell phone at home. She had called his office several times since morning and the only reply she got was that he wasn't there.

The clock kept ticking by and Shanthi started to panic. What if he had gone out in the night to have his dinner and had met with some accident. Was he lying in some hospital unconsciously ? As this thought passed her mind, she was plugged with a gut wrenching fear and she was unable to think coherently. Immediately, she phoned up to her mother and apprised her about the fight she had with her husband last night and also told her that he was missing now. Though her mother was alarmed on hearing this, she calmed her daughter by telling her that nothing untoward would have happened to him and asked her to relax. "Perhaps he might have gone to meet some of his old friends or relatives. Don't worry too much and ruin your health. I shall pray God to ease all your tension. Your husband is sure to return before sunset !" Her mother assured her.

This however did not placate Shanthi's agitation. She kept phoning to all his friends and acquaintances enquiring them if her husband had by chance come over there. Everyone gave her a negative reply. Finally, she spoke to his aunt ; expecting some good news from her. But his aunt was as shocked as she was over his disappearance. She pacified Shanthi by telling her that Swaminathan loved his family so dearly and he was sure to return home during the course of the day.

It was afternoon and Shanthi had not taken her breakfast yet. She was sitting on the sofa in a depressed mood, indulging in vain thoughts. If only her husband returned, she would seek forgiveness from him for being so rude. She was planning to cook a delicious meal for her husband but only after seeing him. When at last she heard the door bell, she strided across the room with her heart in the mouth, praying that it should be her husband. But when she saw her parents and sister, she became disappointed and her spirits fell.

Shanthi's father was quick to observe the unhappy look on his daughter's face and he advised her not to be so upset over this. He further told her that he knew a police inspector and if need arises he could take his assistance in tracing out her husband. Nothing reduced the tension that was building up inside her and Shanthi continued to be restless. On learning that Shanthi had not eaten anything since morning, her mother prepared lunch and forced her to eat, lest she faints.

When Shruthi returned from school, she was excited to see her grandparents. But when she realised that her father was not around, she ran to her mother to find out why her grandparents were here. When Shanthi told her that her father had still not come home, Shruthi began to cry. Everyone fussed over her and allayed her fears that her father would come back and that he had gone to buy a lot of presents for her birthday which was falling next month. But Shruthi was already Eight years old and she could not be easily hoodwinked. She could smell something fishy and sat on her grandmother's lap with tears flowing unceasingly.

As Twilight was turning into night, Shanthi's fears worsened. The police inspector to whom her father had spoken to, called back and confirmed that there had been no report of any accidents in Chennai city last night and hence there was nothing to panic. He also convinced him that his son-in-law might have gone to visit some of his friends and would eventually return and in case of any help, he could feel free to contact him any time.

On seeing her daughter cry, Shanthi was herself moved to tears. Holding her daughter's hand, she went up to the gate. Both mother and daughter stood there for long and when there was no any sign of him, returned dejectedly. They sat down on the steps of the portico, anticipating him.

As Shanthi wiped her daughter's tear stained face with her saree pallu, the face of Nadhiya loomed large in front of her eyes. Nadhiya was the nurse whom Shanthi had befriended in the hospital during her sister's hospitalisation. Shanthi had never seen a smile on her face. Nadhiya always appeared to be gloomy and sad. However, she would carry out all her work with great perfection ; letting no one point a finger at her. But on the day of discharge, Shanthi was quick to notice a transformation in Nadhiya. She was bubbling with excitement and a constant smile kept lingering on her face. As always, Shanthi's curiosity got the better of her and she wished to find out the reason for such a sudden change in her. When the nurse entered the room, Shanthi immediately blurted, "you seem to be in a very pleasant mood today. Anything special ?" As if waiting for such an opportunity, Nadhiya spoke her heart out......

Ten years back, a doctor who was a frequent visitor to this hospital had fallen in love with her. One day, he proposed to her and requested her to marry him. Nadhiya did not have second thoughts and after consultation with her parents consented to marry him. After the wedding was over, both of them took a long leave and went on a honeymoon trip. They returned after a week and were now eager to get back to work.

Nadhiya was busy unpacking her things, when her husband asked her to join him in the open terrace of the second floor. Abandoning her work, Nadhiya trotted behind him and they were involved in a jolly chat. Feeling a little tired, her husband sat down on the narrow parapet wall, while Nadhiya was standing close to him. Suddenly, Nadhiya was attracted by a baby parrot which kept popping its head from a nest on top of a tree adjoining the building. Nadhiya wished to get a better view of the bird and so walked closer to it. In the meanwhile, her husband tried to adjust himself into a more comfortable position, when all of a sudden, he lost his balance and fell off from the parapet wall. Nadhiya rushed towards him on hearing his screams, but could do nothing to stop him from tumbling over. Terrified, she ran down the steps two at a time. On reaching the spot, she was horrified to see her husband lying on the ground unconscious. With the help of her neighbour, Nadhiya rushed him to the hospital and arranged for emergency treatment. Though he survived, he turned into a mere vegetable and had to be confined to the bed for the rest of his life. He had lost all feelings beneath his hip so much so that he was not aware of the natural processes taking place in the lower part of his body. And only when a stinking smell diffused in the air, he would call his wife to clean him up. Nadhiya patiently had been looking after her husband with love and affection all these years. She had not once complained about the horrid life that she had to lead. The fact that her husband was alive and able to talk gladdened her heart. She accepted her fate and did not reproach God for whatever He has done to her. There was no love lost between them after this accident and Nadhiya continued to love her husband even more. She worked hard day in and day out in order to take care of her husband.

And the reason for her happiness now, she confessed to Shanthi with a smile on her face was that a new doctor who had joined the hospital had promised to cure her husband. After this treatment, her husband would be able to sit in a wheel chair and move around.

Shanthi had then listened to Nadhiya with rapt attention and was very much touched by her poignant story. She had all the while been regarding her as a haughty woman with no kind feelings. But after hearing her pathetic story, she was overwhelmed with empathetic feelings towards her...........

With her hands cupping her chin, Shanthi was still sitting in the portico, thinking about Nadhiya. Shanthi felt that the life of that nurse was far better than hers; for she had her husband alive, to whom she could atleast talk and share her feelings. And now Shanthi was not sure of the fate she was going to be meted out with. She was sitting there wallowing in self pity, brooding over her husband.

If only her husband comes back, she would treat him with more kindness and love and never again belittle him!

Shanthi continued sitting in the portico, musing over the turn of events. Rage and panic pounded through her. She was enraged as to why her husband did not keep her informed about his whereabouts. At the same time, she also panicked if something untoward had happened to him due to which he was unable to communicate to her. Suddenly she felt a sick feeling in the pit of her stomach. Where was he now ? What was he doing ? She wanted her husband back ; whatever condition he was in now - a cripple, an invalid or in a state of coma. Her mind was in total chaos. Nothing seemed to calm the jumble of emotions inside her.

Since it was already midnight, Shanthi's mother came out and requested her to have dinner and go to sleep. She further tried to calon by telling her that her husband would have got held up somewhere and would return at his earliest convenience. But Shanthi did not respond to her mother. In fact, she was very much irked by her mother's comforting words; for her mother was in a way responsible for such a predicament. By blindly following in her mother's footsteps, she had wanted to keep her husband completely under her control - so much so that she had given him no freedom; besides nagging him constantly. Though they were husband and wife, they were two different individuals with different feelings, likes and dislikes. And each required a certain distance and freedom between them. Failing to realize this, Shanthi had stretched his patience beyond a certain limit which had made him to leave her. Shanthi was now facing the music of her action.

Despite her mother's coaxing, Shanthi went to bed without having dinner. Mentally exhausted, she closed her eyes but sleep evaded her. She lay there in the dark wishing that atleast by morning, her husband should come back. Hoping for the best, she closed her eyes once again and tried to get some sleep. She woke up earlier than usual and was disappointed that her husband had not returned yet. She began her chores in earnest and finished her work rather too quickly. She then got ready along with her daughter to go to the nearby temple. She wanted to perfom a special puja for her husband's return by evening.

As luck would have it, there was no news about him during the rest of the day nor the next day. It was on the third day that Shanthi's patience was taking a toll over her. However she continued to wait without losing heart ; firmly believing that her husband would return home anytime and give a plausible justification for his absence. When there was no news about him even after a week, Shanthi had an overwhelming sense that something terrible was going to happen to her. For the first time, eversince his disappearance, Shanthi came to a conclusion that her husband had left her ; unable to bear her nitpicking character.

However, Shanthi was determined not to get bogged down by this. She wished to face the realities of life with courage. With a strong mind, she decided to start a new life ; for she did not wish that her daughter be affected by her depressed mood. By reserving the pain and sorrow over her husband's missing to herself, she put on a false pretense in front of her daughter. Shruthi was the only comfort to her now. Her entire life revolved around her daughter. Unlike before, she treated her with more kindness. She stopped sending her to tuition and started teaching her. Her daughter's presence gave her some solace.

While Shruthi rejoiced in her mother's affection and pampering, a strong feeling was etched in her mind that it was because of her mother that her father had left the house. However, being too young she did not either question her mother about this nor hold any grudge against her. Many a times, Shanthi would see her standing near the window ; blankly staring at the road. Immediately, Shanthi would go and hug her daughter lovingly. Shruthi would then ask her pathetically, "Ma, will father come back to us or no ?" Shanthi would assure her that he was sure to come back and that very soon they were going to be a happy and close knit family.

Shanthi went about all her activities, living in the moment and not thinking beyond the moment. She had often heard people say that things happened to people as they were destined to happen and that it was not possbile to change one's Fate. Shanthi too had all the while believed in this concept. But now, her views on this differed. For she was in no way going to accept the Fate that God had handed out to her. She was going to fight with Him and bring back her husband. Was not God above Fate and if so, she was determined to win over her Fate through her fervent prayers.

Night and day Shanthi performed special pujas to God. She prayed for two things. One is that her husband should be alive somewhere and the other is that he should come back sooner or later. Her prayers gave her confidence and she went about her daily activities without getting disgusted with life. Though she was heartbroken over her husband's desertion, she tried not to lose her balance.

Shanthi's family continued to stay with her. Her parents were bent on tracing out her husband and uniting him with her. They were not willing to leave her alone when she was in sorrow.

A week before Priya's admission to the hospital, her paternal uncle visited them in connection with settlement of her marriage. Her father who was already in the look out for a suitable boy for her was indeed happy to hear the news. At once, he contacted his eldest daughter, who was a pillar of strength to him and conveyed the matter. Further, he requested her to make necessary arrangements for a meeting with the bridegroom's family. Shanthi was delighted to hear the news and she agreed to help him. In coordination with her uncle, she fixed up a day for the boy-seeing-girl function. On the D-day, the whole family received the bridegroom with great cheerfulness. Shanthi alongwith Valli, the live-in servant maid had organised everything for the occasion. Shanthi helped her mother in preparing refreshments for the guests and also embellished her sister with all her ornaments. She further goaded her not to be shy and talk boldly when being questioned either by the bridegroom or his family members.

Finally, after giving a send off to the bridegroom's family, Shanthi turned to Priya to seek her opinion about the bridegroom. With curiosity writ large on her face, she asked Priya if she liked the boy. Priya just smiled and did not say anything. However, Shanthi was quick to notice the blush on her face and had taken her silence as a sign of assent. It was during this moment when all were eagerly waiting for a response from the bridegroom's family that Priya suddenly fell ill and had to be hospitalised. Immediately after her return from the hospital, Shanthi had picked up a quarrel with Swaminathan, resulting in their separation. After this, Shanthi was so depressed in life and almost forgot about this issue.

One evening, a week after Swaminathan abandoned her, Shanthi was sitting in the portico, plaiting her daughter's hair when her cell phone buzzed. With her heart in her mouth, she picked it up ; expecting some news about her husband. But on hearing her uncle's voice, her spirits fell. Brimming with excitement, he informed her that the bridegroom's family at last had given their concurrence with regard to the alliance. He was not aware of her mental anguish for Shanthi was very particular that this matter be kept a secret. She had also strictly instructed Shruthi not to reveal this to anybody and if someone asked her about her father, all that she had to tell was that he had gone abroad in connection with a new job. Unmindful of her sorry plight, her uncle continued to speak to her with great zeal. He advised her to consult an astrologer first and fix up a date for the betrothal and marriage functions. Shanthi had in fact been skeptical about the fruition of this marriage as there had been no feedback from them for more than a month. She was now glad to hear the good news despite her low spirits. Promising him that she would communicate everything to her father and get back to him soon, she went in to share the news with her family.

Eversince Swaminathan left the house, Priya had been devastated. The fact that she had been the cause of their fight made her feel rather uncomfortable in front of her sister. She remained gloomy all the time. In fact, she was seething with anger over her sister's debase attitude in connecting her husband with her. However, she remained taciturn and did not question her ; for she had been the one who had lovingly taken care of her in the hospital.

When Shanthi broke the news to Priya, she was not happy at all. Afterall, what joy would it give her to get married at a time when her sister's life was in doldrums. Curtly she told her sister, "what is the hurry for my marriage now ? Ask them to wait for a few months. I do not like to get married at this point of time when the whole family is engulfed in sadness !" Supporting her views, her father enjoined, "what Priya says is right. We must ask them to wait for a while until Swaminathan's return. It would not be appropriate to conduct the wedding during his absence. What reply would I give to people when they ask me about my Son-in-Law ?"

Shanthi was rather cut up on hearing her father's justification regarding postponement of her sister's wedding. She was not for either delaying the marriage unduly or cancelling it on account of her plight. In fact she did not wish to carry a guilt bag for the rest of her life. Looking at her sister, she asked, "for how long do you all plan to wait for my husband's return ? He has not gone on any official tour after giving me his tour itinerary so that we can all be sure of his imminent arrival and hence wait for his return. I am ofcourse praying God earnestly and am confident that He will not let me down. Right now, I have no choice except to wait for him patiently. Postponing the marriage indefinitely until his return is a foolish decision. I feel that we should not let such an opportunity slip out of our hands and it would be only right that we go ahead with the marriage !" There was a long spell of silence for no one dared to argue with her further.

Shanthi was in fact grieving the loss of her relationship with her husband and was still reeling from shock over the sudden change of events in her life. At times, she could not believe that such a thing happened to her and would wonder if she was having a nightmare. However, she did not wish to keep brooding over this all the time and be an object of pity.

Instead, in a very courageous manner, she tried to come out of her gloominess. The betrothal and the marriage functions of her sister were indeed a good distraction to her at the apt time. The following days were hectic for Shanthi. She involved herself in the arrangements of the function and went out frequently on a shopping spree in connection with the wedding. This temporarily brought her out of her melancholy.

However, during the nights Shanthi would lie in the dark, wide awake reminiscing about all the illtreatment she had meted out to her husband. She was aware that she had in fact taken too much advantage over his lenient nature and behaved in an overbearing manner. Now, God was punishing her for her vicious character and all she could do was to meekly accept His punishment without murmuring.

She felt sorry for her husband. If only he was in front of her right now, she would plead guilty for all the wrong she had done to him and also promise him that she would turn over a new leaf. At times, she would keep hallucinating that her husband should somehow get wind of her sister's marriage and surprise her by popping up in front of her on the wedding day.

Shruthi tried to come out of the situation by clinging on to her grandparents who showered their love on her. She was also very happy that her grandparents and aunt continued to stay with them. Being a sharp witted girl, she was quick to realize that whenever she asked her mother about her father, she would become morose for the rest of the day. Not wishing to see her mother in a sulky mood, she slowly stopped pestering her as to when her father would return.

Even at school, she stopped talking to all her friends suddenly ; for she did not like to be in the midst of girls who bragged about their dads. Instead, she made friends with Saranya, who was a new comer to her class that year. Saranya was a reserved girl and hardly spoke to anyone. But what attracted Shruthi to her was that, just like her, she was also fatherless. Day after day, their friendship grew by leaps and bounds and they became very close to each other.

As the wedding day of her aunt was fast approaching, Shruthi looked so thrilled. She merrily went out shopping with her mother. She felt joyous by the fact that unlike before, her mother never scolded her and bought her everything that she asked for. When she told her mother that she wished to invite her best friend for the wedding, Shanthi readily obliged. Shruthi was beaming from ear to ear as she accompanied her mother to Saranya's house to invite them.

As expected, during the marriage function, Shanthi's relatives kept pounding her with questions about her husband's absence and Shanthi deftly handled the situation by telling them that her husband had just joined a new company in Dubai a month ago and hence was not in a position to take leave.

At last, when it was time for Priya to take leave, she broke down. Apart from having to leave her family, Priya was feeling sorry for her sister, who despite her sadness, had been solely responsible for materialisation of this marriage. But for her coercing and changing her mind, the marriage would either have got prolonged unduly or cancelled.

As soon as Priya was gone, her parents were overwhelmed with sadness. While they were happy over their younger daughter's marriage, they were distressed by their elder daughter's fate, for there had been no news about Swaminathan yet. Further, they were in a fix and not sure whether to return to their house or continue staying with their daughter till her husband's return.

It was during this time that Shanthi took a wise decision. Being a home maker, Shanthi suddenly felt that all her savings had dwindled after Swaminathan had left her. She did not like that she be a burden to her father by depending on his meagre pension every month. She decided to rent her house and move along with her parents. She filled in the lacunae left behind by Priya.

On the other hand, Shruthi was much excited about her change of place, for it was quite nearby to her school. Daily shruthi enjoyed walking to school with her grandfather. She spent her leisure time with her grandparents. Her new friendship that she developed at school with Saranya and the change of place, slowly made her forget her father. Shanthi was pleased to see the transformation that came about in her daughter.

Though Shruthi was only in the fourth standard, her portions were too heavy. Shanthi had gone to a school with State Board syllabus and hence she was finding her daughter's Central Board pattern rather too difficult. Shanthi had to first of all do a lot of homework before teaching her.

One evening, Shanthi was sitting with her daughter, helping her do the maths homework, when all of a sudden, Valli, her live-in servant maid came and sat down beside her. Valli had been of great help to her family for almost fifteen years now. Even during Priya's wedding, Valli had exerted herself so much so that, Shanthi pleased with her services, promised to increase her salary after talking to her father. Now, presuming that Valli had come to speak to her about this, Shanthi apologised, "I have still not discussed with father about your pay hike. Please give me some ...."

"Oh ! I have not come for asking you about my rise in salary." Valli interrupted. "I want to discuss another important issue with you. The time has come for me to leave you all !"

Shanthi was jolted and she asked, "What makes you take such a drastic decision ? Have you got a better job somewhere ?"

Valli shook her head. "No no ! How can I leave you people and go elsewhere ? Your family had given me a new lease of life and had supported me when I was in dire need of help !"

As Shanthi sat there wondering what exactly could be the reason for her leaving them, Valli continued, "my man is coming to take me back to the village. His term of imprisonment is over and I am left with no option but to simply accompany him."

Shanthi was dumbfounded. For it was Valli, who had taken care of all the household chores thus enabling everyone to have ample of time on their hands to pursue with their interests. It was not going to be an easy task to find a replacement for her. Not wanting her to go, Shanthi asked, "can't your husband find some job here in Chennai itself ? That way you can still continue to work for us."

Valli was not very keen to continue her stay in Chennai. To her, Chennai was indeed the best city to make some money if you really cared to do hard work. She had also never been in paucity of funds eversince she landed in Chennai. However, she reasoned that money was not everything in life. Somehow, she felt that Chennai was not a lucky place for her. First, she had lost her loving son and then her husband was also forced to leave her. Valli was not willing to go back to the village then. For she did not wish to be a burden to her father who had to get her younger sisters married as well. Besides, with a view to support him financially, she continued to stay all alone in Chennai. Now, she wished to go back and settle down in her village ; for that is where her roots were. She wished to start over a new life along with her husband ; forgetting the dreadful past. More than anythingelse, she was yearning to have a baby.

As Shanthi stared at her agape ; curious about the reply she was going to give, Valli said, "Chennai has not been a lucky place for both of us. We had to lead separate lives. Hence, I wish to go back to my village and start a new life in the midst of my relatives. I am sure that my husband would behave well and also treat me kindly when elders are around."

Shanthi was however astounded by the fact as to how it was possible for Valli to forgive her husband who was the murderer of her son. Not reserving her thoughts to herself, she blurted, "Howcome you have decided to go back with that man who had killed your son in anger ?"

Valli was rather quick to respond, "whatelse can I do ? After all there is just one life for us to live. There is no point in taking endless revenge on him. Moreover, I also plan to have a baby and start over a new life erasing the horrible past from my mind. I have already wasted half of my life and do not wish to do so with the rest of my life."

Shanthi realised that nothing she said was going to change her mind. For Valli was steadfast in her decision to go back to her village.

Shanthi was disappointed by Valli's decision to leave them. Valli had been part of her family and had shared in the happy and sad moments of her life. Even now, whenever she was in a gloomy mood, Valli would hold her hand lovingly and assure her, "my words will always turn out to be true. Wait and see, your husband is going to come back very soon and surprise you all !" Just thinking of those kind words brought tears to Shanthi now. She was indeed going to miss Valli and her guileless speech very badly.

Everyone in the family were sad on hearing the news about Valli's return to her village. Parvathi was the one who was most affected by this. Valli had been the right hand to her who had assisted her in all the household chores eversince Shanthi was a child. Valli's leaving nearly broke her heart. She very well knew that finding a replacement for her was going to be a difficult task.

When at last the time of Valli's departure arrived, the whole family gathered to give her a send off. As Parvathi handed over some money and a few old sarees to her, she said, "keep visiting us from time to time and don't forget to inform us when you are blessed with a child." Valli silently stood there nodding her head. She was herself overwhelmed with sadness at having to part from this family after having worked here for such a long time. She was also not sure how this new life was chalked out for her. Valli was finding it very hard to suppress the tears that welled up in her eyes. Suddenly, she bent down and after picking up her bag and baggages started walking slowly towards the bus stand, where her husband was waiting for her ; all the while wiping the incessant tears that kept flowing from her eyes. Another chapter had come to an end.

After giving send off to Valli, Shanthi despondently walked into the house which seemed to have a deserted look now. There was dreariness all around and everyone missed Valli's boisterous voice. That night as Shanthi went to bed, she lay awake for a long time ruminating over Valli. How easily had Valli forgiven her husband. Does time assuage everything in life ? The anger, hatred, vengeance one harbors against another ? If that was true, then her husband too would eventually forgive her and return home one day. This optimistic thought enriched her with a new ray of hope. Would she also be able to see sunshine in her life ? If so, when was that going to be ? This was the question that begged for an answer.

As expected, despite her best efforts, Shanthi was unable to find a replacement to Valli. At last, she gave up her search and decided to take up the additional responsibility of household chores as well. After cooking the meals, she washed the dishes and clothes by herself. She was also a nurse to her parents and gave them medicines from time to time. Apart fom these, she was a tutor to her daughter too. She spent some time in the evenings with her, clearing all her doubts. However, in the midst of these activities, she did not forget her prayers to God. Shanthi was occupied with one job or the other from dawn to dusk. It was this busy life style coupled with her prayers that kept her turbulant mind rather calm.

It was six months since her husband had left her and yet there was no any news from him. As if this was not enough, Valli too had left the family ; leaving her with the additional burden of household chores. Shanthi however did not allow herself to become weak by these circumstances. Instead, she derived even more strength out of the whole crisis.

Beyond our personal screams and tears, life moves on. Shanthi realised that she now had a responsibility towards her other relationships. There was no point in dwelling too much on her husband, a relationship which she had lost for now. By constantly thinking of him, she would not be able to do justice to her daughter. Suddenly, she was thankful to God for atleast having her daughter - someone to love and in turn be loved. She had to help her grow.

The days slowly passed into months and the months into years. The wheel of time took a fast turn and Shruthi entered the tenth standard. The fact that her daughter was going to appear for the Board

Examination filled Shanthi with tension. She kept advising her to study hard and score good marks. "If you score good marks, you can choose the course you want to study. On the other hand, if you score less, you have to rest content with whatever subject you are offered." She said. Shruthi took her mother's advice rather seriously. She set a target of getting Ninety Percent in all the subjects and thus please her mother. Night and Day, she kept studying and at last her hard work met with success for she was able to achieve her goal. While Shanthi was reveling over her daughter's results, another crisis was looming large in front of her. Shanthi was utterly confused and was not sure as to how she was going to tackle this new problem that was confronting her.

Saranya, Shruthi's best friend scored only Seventy Five percent in the Board Examination. Her mother wanted her to become an Engineer and hence she decided to put her in Fathima Higher Secondary School, which followed the State Board syllabus. This would enable her daugther to score better marks in her Plus Two Examination and thus getting admission into reputed Engineering Colleges through counselling, without shelling out a lot of money would become easy. When Saranya conveyed the news about her change of school to Shruthi, she became very upset. Immediately Saranya told her, "well, if you wish, you can also join the new school and we can then continue our friendship." Shruthi at once decided to oblige her friend. She too was willing to change her school along with Saranya. But before this, she had to first of all get her mother's consent.

On reaching home, she ran to her mother and expressed her desire regarding the change of school.

But her mother was against this. Shruthi then started pestering her mother by telling her that she would be missing her friend very badly and hence wanted to go along with her. Shanthi tried to convince her, "your friend is leaving the school because she is finding the Central Board Syllabus very difficult. But this is not the case with you. You have secured Ninety Two percent and with some extra coaching, you will be able to get even better marks in your Plus Two Exams." However, Shruthi was not satisfied with her mother's explanation. She started justifying to her mother, "years back, when I had made friends with Saranya, both of us took an vow that we would never part from each other and remain life long friends. Now, Saranya is coaxing me also to join the new school and I do not wish to refuse." Shanthi said rather curtly, "you can still continue to be her best friend. Both of you can meet during weekends and on holidays." But Shruthi was adamant and was not willing to take a "No" for an answer. Silently she walked away from there with a grumpy face.

She switched on the television and sat down in front of it. She kept flipping the channels one after another and finally decided to watch a movie to keep off from tension. She sat there watching the film without any interest. Actually, she was in a sulky mood and wished to avoid her mother.

In the afternoon, after Shanthi finished her cooking, she came and requested her to have lunch. But Shruthi refused by telling that she was not feeling hungry and carelessly continued watching TV. Though Shanthi realised that she was lying to her, she did not wish to start an argument with her and hence left the place without another word. But when Shruthi did not have her lunch until 3.00 p.m. she became angry and shouted, "are you going to have your lunch now or not ?" Shruthi once again gave her the same reply that she was not feeling hungry. Shanthi knew pretty well that her daughter was showing her hostility towards her for not acceding to her request of change of school.

It was only now that Shanthi repented. She had spoiled her daughter by giving in to all her demands just because she was growing up without her father by her side. Suddenly Shanthi feared that her refusal to comply with her request might end-up in a misunderstanding between mother and daughter. Shanthi did not wish that such a thing should happen. Afterall, her whole life revolved on the happiness of her daughter. Finally, she called her daughter and said, "I know that you are lying to me that you are not hungry. Don't starve like this unnecessarily. First come and have your food. If you are so desirous and firm about changing your school, act as you please. I am not going to stand on the way !"

Shruthi's face immediately lit up with a bright smile. Giving her a bear-hug she said, "thank you so much Ma. I have the best mother in this world !" She then accompanied her to the dining hall and ate up the food her mother served her in a voracious manner ; all the while thanking her for her kindness in yielding to her request.

The next morning, Shanthi went to meet the principal alongwith Shruthi to obtain the Transfer Certificate as the same was required at the time of seeking admission to the new school. After hearing out Shanthi patiently, the principal became rather furious and said, "perhaps you might have seen the crowd outside my office. They are anxious parents waiting to meet me in connection with admission of their children into this prestigious school and here you are requesting me for a Transfer Certificate. What makes you take such a drastic decision ?" Shanthi then explained her predicament to her. She told her that it was her daughter who was so stubborn in leaving the school and she had no say in the matter. Infuriated by this, she said, "you cannot give me such a callous reply. As a parent, it is your duty to advise her in a proper manner. She is too young to take right decisions now."

Shanthi was tongue tied and after a moment of silence she said, "you are indeed right madam. But these days, children are very unrelenting and hardly obey their parents. I had in fact tried my best in changing her mind but she is very steadfast in her decision of leaving the school and I am helpless."

"Well, if your decision to leave the school is final, please come along with her father tomorrow. As per the rules and regulations of this school, the Transfer Certificate will be given only in the presence of both the parents."

Shanthi was now stupefied. She then told her the same lie that she had been telling everyone that her father was in Dubai and he would not be able to take leave and come right away. This further aroused the principal's anger and she yelled, "so what ? Ask him to come down here and collect the TC if he feels that his daughter's education is important. I cannot disregard the rules of the school for I am answerable to my superiors."

Shanthi continued to sit there staring at her pleadingly but the Principal only said, "please try to understand my position. My hands are tied and I cannot violate the rules for the sake of just one student. By doing so, every other parent will come to me for favouring them out of the way. So, please ask her father also to come for collecting the Transfer Certificate."

Shanthi got up and left the place in a huff. She knew that anything she said was not going to change the Principal's mind.

Both mother and daughter walked back home in silence not sure of the next step that had to be taken.

Back home, Shanthi asked her daughter, "now tell me what am I suppose to do ?' Though Shruthi knew that her mother was helpless, she was angry with her. Afterall, it was because of her that her father had left the house. In a rude manner, she said, "from the beginning, you were against my leaving this school ! it is your wish that has got fulfilled at last. Now, I am going to miss my friend a lot."

She then walked away from there and lay down on the bed crying. She had all along got things done her way. She could not face the failures of life.

"Stop crying now !" Shanthi came in pacifying her. "I shall talk to the higherups in the school management and see that you get your Transfer Certificate. Just give me some time !" Shruthi's face immediately lit up with a smile on her mother's reassurance. For she was sure that her mother would keep up her words.

However, when a week had passed by and her mother had not initiated any action regarding this, she started to worry as to what was holding her back. It was a Thursday morning and Shanthi was doing her usual puja when the phone rang. Since her mother would not attend to any calls nor speak to anyone while she was in the midst of her prayer, Shruthi ran to pick up the phone. She was amazed to hear Saranya's voice. Saranya had called to remind her that there were just three days left for submission of application forms and wished to know if she was joining the new school or not. Shruthi pathetically informed her that she was yet to obtain the transfer certificate and promised to get back to her by evening.

Suddenly, Shruthi's spirits fell. She became concerned over her mother's lackadaisical attitude and hence decided to break the ice today. She went and stood beside her mother with a sullen face. Once her mother was done with her puja, she slowly began, "Ma, Saranya is asking me to hurry up as there are just three days left for submission of application forms."

Shanthi had herself been breaking her head night and day as to whom to meet in this regard. While offering her prayers to God today, she wholeheartedly beseeched upon Him to show her the way. Now, seeing the tension writ large on her daughter's face, she tried to assuage her anxiety. "Well, that means we have another Seventy Two hours left and anything could happen within this time. Just relax and be cool. Today, I will somehow solve your problem." As she said this, she heard the door bell chime. She went to find out who it was; with Shruthi trailing behind her gloomily. When Shanthi opened the door, she was jolted. Ramanathan was standing there brimming with a smile. She stood there agape, without even inviting him in. On seeing her alarming expression, Ramanathan asked, "both mother and daughter look so awful. Have I intruded any serious discussion that you were having?" It was only then that Shanthi realised her folly and asked him to come in. In fact, Shanthi was too happy to see him and believed that it was God who had sent him at the appropriate time to help her out. For Ramanathan had contacts with many big shots in the locality and Shanthi was confident that he would get the Transfer Certificate from the school by hook or by crook.

With a smile lingering on her face, Shanthi offered him a glass of water and said, "you are indeed right ! Shruthi is very upset right now. She has just finished her tenth standard Board Examination in Jawahar School. One of her best friends is joining Fathima Higher Secondary School and Shruthi too wants to go along with her. But her principal is refusing to give her the Transfer Certificate and insists that her father's presence is also required at the time of handing over the TC.

Ramanathan felt a spurt of satisfaction on hearing her predicament. He patted himself on his back for he had come here at the right time in sorting out her problem. All these years Shanthi had been lying to him that her husband was in Dubai and hence Ramanathan wished to take her to task for this. He decided to prolong his disclosure regarding his purpose of visit for a little while and have some fun. He began his play-acting.

Suppressing all his emotions, he said, "well, you can phone up to her father and ask him to come down here immediately. Afterall, he also has a certain amount of responsibility towards his daughter !"

Shanthi winced on hearing these words and became dumbfounded. She was caught red handed and was now paying heavily for having duped him all these years. She did not wish to spin another tale and further deceive him. She realised that now was the apt time to divulge the truth to him. For only then will he be able to assist her in a befitting manner. Slowly, she let the cat out of the bag.

"I have been hiding a fact from you all these years!" she said sadly. "In fact, I had been lying to you all the while that my husband is working in Dubai. But actually, the truth is that we could not get along smoothly. I had taken things for granted and kept bossing over him for each and everything. One day, he left the house after a quarrel, as much as without a word with me. I am not sure where he has gone. In fact I even don't know if he is alive or not....."

As she uttered these words, tears sprang up to her eyes and Shanthi covered her face with her saree pallu to wipe away her tears.

On seeing her cry, Ramanathan was swept away by an wave of pity and his heart suddenly melted. Forgetting his resolve, he blurted, "don't worry about that. He is very much alive !"

Paralysed in shock, Shanthi stared at him in disbelief. Looking at his serious expression, she realised that he was not joking. Her heart started pounding against her ribs and she was unable to think coherantly. Shaken up by his words, she babbled, "what did you say just now ? My husband is alive ? Did you really see him ?"

Ramanathan gave a nod and said, "yes of course, I met Swaminathan a few days back !"

Shanthi was flabbergasted and she started harrying him with questions one after another. "When did you meet him ? Where is he now ?"

"I saw him in Kanchipuram and he apprised me of everything. He told me that unable to bear with your frequent bickerings and reproaches he was ultimately forced to leave ; seeking some retreat in life. However he expressed his sadness and guilty feelings at backing down from his marriage commitment and was missing his daughter too......"

Interrupting him, Shanthi asked with great concern in her voice, "Why did you not ask him to come back home ?"

"I did request him. But he is scared out of his wits. He is not sure if you would accept him back in to your life for having ditched you like that. Finally, I told him that you were not such a heartless person and assured him that I would act as a go between to unite him with his family. I was suppose to meet him yesterday morning with all of you. But due to my memory lapse, I just forgot all about it. Since you had been lying to me all these years, I wished to take you for a ride and hence did not divulge the purpose of my visit in the beginning itself. But when I saw you cry, I could not continue with my enactment. Actually, I have come here on a mission to bring both of you together. Now, go and get ready quickly and I shall take you to meet him." Then turning to Shruthi he asked, "haven't I solved your problem young lady ?" I am going to bring back your father. Promise me that you will be a loving daughter to him." Shruthi silently stood there grinnng at him.

Shanthi was too exhilarated and could not believe the sudden turn of events that was to occur in her life. Was she having a nice dream ? She pinched herself several times to check if whatever she was hearing was real. She then ran to convey the news to her parents. Pumping her fists into the air she said excitedly, “at last God has answered my prayers ! My husband is alive and we are going to see him rightaway!”

It was 10.00 a.m when the whole family arrived in Kanchipuram. Ramanathan decided to take them directly to the temple hoping to find Swaminathan there, as there was still time left to close the temple. But on reaching the temple, he became upset on finding it locked. Perhaps, Swaminathan was rather shy to meet his family members in the attire of a priest and must have stayed back at home, he thought. With this view, he started walking towards his house. However, he asked Shanthi to stay back in the temple itself for he wished to bring about their union in the presence of Lord Vinayagar. But when he found that the house was also locked, he was baffled.

Doubts began to assail his mind. Has Swaminathan absconded once again not willing to join his family ? And was it because of his coaxing that he had agreed to come back home ?

Perplexed, he knocked at the landlord’s house. When the old man came out, he asked, “could you please tell me where Swaminathan has gone ?”

The old man said, “he has left this place already. The whole of yesterday, he was expecting a friend of his who had promised him a job in Chennai. When that person did not turn up, he decided to go and meet him personally and hence left for Chennai early in the morning.”

It was only then that Ramanathan heaved a sigh of relief ! He now became optimistic for he very well knew that Swaminathan must have been in fact waiting for him. Probably, his insinuatng speech he had had with him regarding his entry into family life again must have had a tremendous effect on him so much so that he was too eager to join his family. That's why when he was unable to keep his promise of meeting him yesterday, he should have decided to return to his family on his own. Hoping for the best, he thanked the old man and turned to leave.

However, Ramanathan was disappointed by the fact that it was all due to his lackadaisical attitude that had resulted in such a chaos. If only he had met him yesterday morning, as per his promise, things would have got straightened out by now. He returned with a sullen face ; cursing his wife all the way. For she was the main cause for such a disarray........

Though Ramanathan intended to return home on Monday night, he could not make it ; for his conversation with Swaminathan extended far beyond midnight. It was only at 1.30 a.m that he was able to come back to his hotel. He was too fatigued by then and immediately fell asleep. On Tuesday morning, he woke up at 10.00 a.m and wondered if he was in the middle of a desert, for the sun was blazing down like hell. Fearing the scorching sun, which might trigger his migraine, he decided to check out of the hotel only in the evening.

As he entered his house that night, he saw his wife preparing a hot meal for him. Sniffing the aroma that swept across in the air, he walked into the kitchen and handed over his bag to her and went to have a wash. When he returned afresh, Gowri served him dinner, beaming with a smile and enquiring about his trip. Ramanathan greedily started gorging his food as he was famished. He loved his wife's cooking so much so that whenever he went out on such religious tours, he really missed her a lot. He told her about the various temples he had visited and chided her for not accompanying him.

Unlike her husband, Gowri did not believe in these religious tours which Ramanathan was so fond of making every year. She held that God was in the hearts of people around you and tried to be kind with everyone who approached her. However, when it came to her husband, she was losing her patience of late. It was mostly due to his memory loss which was getting on her nerves.

After serving him dinner, Gowri started exploring the contents of the bag which he had given her. Before leaving for Kanchipuram, she had requested him to buy a silk saree which she wished to give as gift to her Daughter-In-Law during her visit to Bangalore in the Summer vacation. As she kept rummaging the bag, her enthusiasm began to sag concomittantly building up her tension. For all she could find in it were coconuts, bananas, dried betel leaves, flowers and packets of vhibuthi and vermillion powders. In an agitated mood, she stomped across to the hall and with her hands over her hips yelled, "where is the silk saree that I asked you to buy ?" Ramanathan was for a moment startled by her towering voice. Actually, he had been thinking of buying one after his chat with Swaminathan. However, he became too involved in his story and the shopping he intended to do skipped out of his mind.

Accepting his fault, he grinned sheepishly. "I totally got distracted by the conversation I was having with Swaminathan" He said. He then started narrating the story of his chance meeting with Swaminathan. Forgetting the issue at hand, Gowri was enthralled by his story and she was all ears to him. "I was appalled to know that he had left Shanthi, unable to cope with her nagging character and all the while, Shanthi had been deluding me that her husband was working in Dubai. Finally, I assuaged his anger and hatred he was harboring against his wife and promised to act as a mediator in uniting them. In fact, Wednesday being an auspicious day, I plan to go and meet Shanthi early in the morning tomorrow and apprise her about the meeting I had with her husband. Later, I would be proceeding to Kanchipuram along with her family."

Just as Ramanathan was lauding himself for the great deed he was about to do and also felt a momentary happiness at having deflected his wife's anger over the silk saree, Gowri blasted at him, "tomorrow morning, we are going to Nalli Silk House to purchase a silk saree ! You may meet her in the afternoon and talk to her......"

But Ramanathan was quick to interrupt, "Can't your shopping spree be postponed for a few more days ? Afterall, there is still time left for you to go to Bangalore and I shall definitely buy one before that !"

"No way !" She said rather curtly. "First try to keep your wife happy ! You can than make others happy. After all, Shanthi had been without her husband for six long years and waiting for another day would make no difference in her life !"

On Wednesday morning, Ramanathan accompanied his wife to Nalli Silk House and purhcased her two silk sarees. They returned home at 2.00 p.m. after their shopping spree. Immediately after having his lunch, Ramanathan's head started pounding. He realised that it was all due to roaming in the hot sun and all he could think of was his medical kit. As he popped his pain killers, he instructed his wife, "don't bother me until I wake up on my own. I have taken my migraine pills and do not like to be disturbed." It was 7.00 p.m. when Ramanathan woke up. He got up and walked up to the hall groggily. His wife was fully immersed in her evening soap operas. Ramanathan detested watching these shows and usually chose this hour of the day to be away from home. He would go out walking with his friends. But today, he decided to skip his ritual as he was extremely tired and sat down beside her and started watching the serials along with her.

Early on Thursday morning, Ramanathan was reading the newspaper when Gowri called out to him to come and have his breakfast. Dropping his newspaper on the sofa, he went in. She served him hot idlies with coconut chutney and Ramanathan started relishing them. As he kept devouring the soft idlies one after another, he asked, "today the coconut chutney seems to be very tasty. What did you do ?"

Brimming with a smile, she said, "I did nothing. I prepared it in the same usual manner. I used the tender coconuts that you brought from Kanchipuram and perhaps that could be the cause for its extra flavour."

The moment Gowri uttered the word Kanchipuram, Ramanathan was jolted. Patting his forehead several times, he stood up immediately ; as usual cursing himself for his poor memory. It was only now that he remembered about Swamianthan and the promise he had made to him that he would be meeting him along with his family on Wednesday. He regretted that he could not keep his promise. As he rushed to wash his soiled hands, he shouted at Gowri, "can't you do something about my amnesia ? It is getting from bad to worse these days. Yesterday, after I returned from shopping, I intended to go and meet Shanthi but could not do so due to my headache. However, I decided to meet her in the evening but forgot all about it and cooly sat beside you watching TV. At least you could have reminded me about that. Afterall, you often keep bragging yourself to be young and energetic !"

Handing over a towel to him, Gowri rejoined, "well, now stop scolding me. It was you who told me not to disturb you. And finally when you woke up in the evening, I was by then so much engrossed with the reel life drama and forgot all about your real life drama!" Her evasive reply only infuriated him. Seeing that his face was writ large in anger, she tried to placate his mood. "Well, I did not think that amnesia could be infectious ! Now stop yelling at me and go and meet Shanthi righaway ; lest you forget all about it once again." She said. This brought a smile on his face and wiping his hands with the towel she was holding out for him, Ramanathan said, "after apprising Shanthi about the facts, I shall be proceeding to Kanchipuram if everything goes out smoothly. I shall be late for lunch." He then rushed out of the house...........

Now walking back to the temple he kept repenting about the lapse on his part. If only his wife had not been so obstinate in carrying out her shopping, things would have got straightened out by now. Gowri had disrupted all his plans and hence cursing her all the way, he reached the temple in a dejected mood.

When Shanthi saw him returning alone, she became skeptical. Why was her husband not accompanying him? Was he not willing to see her ? Or worse yet has he once again absconded not willing to get into family life. Reserving her doubts to herself, she stood there with her heart in her mouth. Shruthi too was lingering around restlessly. Eversince Ramanathan told her that he was going to bring back her father, she was too much exhilarated. For now, there was going to be no problem with regard to obtaining her transfer certificate. However, when she saw him return alone, without her father, her spirits fell and she became sullen too.

At last, when Ramanathan approached them, everyone anxiously peered into his face for any cue about what he was going to say. Cutting a sorry figure, Ramanathan said, "first of all, I wish to apologize to all of you for creating such a confusion. It is all due to my lackadaisical attitude that such a chaos has occurred. I was actually suppose to meet Swamnathan yesterday with all of you. However, due to certain exigencies I could not carry out my plan. I was informed by the landlord that Swaminathan had been waiting for me the whole of yesterday and has left for Chennai this morning."

In order to cheer up Shanthi, he further continued teasingly, "perhaps he is too eager to get back to his family and must have left on his own, making my job as a mediator redundant. Let us now hurry up and return to Chennai so as not to disappoint him further."

This however did not change Shanthi's mood. She continued to be tensed. Hoping that things would turn out for the better, she slowly walked towards the busstand.

Abandoning his family was an unexpected twist in Swaminathan's life. However, he tried to turn his despair into freedom by being close to God. For he believed that God excused all your sins, even if the laws of earth demand that you suffer the consequences of the crime.

Eversince Swaminathan had left his family, he was filled with pangs of guilt. However, he was of the opinion that if he wholeheartedly repented in front of God, He was sure to forgive all his sins. ....

When the old landlord had requested him to take up the additional responsiblity of working as a Priest in the Vinayagar Temple, Swaminathan had at first turned down the offer as he detested the same. He evaded his request by telling him that he was not well versed with the procedure of performing the puja in a temple. But the old man was not willing to let go off easily. He persisted that it was not an arduous task and all he had to do was learn a few slokas. Further, he handed over some books and asked him to by heart a few slokas that he had marked.

Swaminathan was sitting in his room all alone memorizing the slokas disinterestingly when all of a sudden, his eyes fell on a glossy yellow colour book. He took the book and started leafing through the pages. The subject interested him and he continued reading the book until he came to the following sentence :

"Anger, greed, desire, pride, sex originate only by way of attachment. With no attachment, you become free of all these evils. Gradually you become a free soul and do not remain bound by your surroundings any more."

He immediately closed the book and began pondering over it at great length. Was it all God's doing ? Was it His intention that he lead a life of seclusion and non attachment ?

Even as a young boy, he had lost both his parents on the same day. But God had not let him down completely for he got love and affection from his aunt. Though initially he had cried in grief everyday, eventually he had come out of it. He adapted to his new life in his aunt's house. By minding to his own business and being helpful to his aunt, he had lived with her until his marriage.

He was joyfully looking forward to his new relationship after marriage. But very soon, the truth staggered him. The fact that he was married to a nagging woman worried him. He accepted whatever God had given him and silently went about his life. But after the birth of Shruthi, when he saw that Shanthi was giving vent to her anger by hiting his beloved daughter, he started losing his temper. He was finding it hard to control himself and he feared that he might also turn as wild as his father and do some nasty thing. One fine day, he walked out of her life without as much as a word to anyone - for his own good and for the good of his family.

He re-read the sentence several times for it brought solace to his rather confused mind. Perhaps it was God's desire that he lead a spiritual life bereft of any attachments. His mind now became clear of all the doubts that had been plugging him and he took up the job of Priest in the Vinayagar Temple in good earnest and faith. If he was destined for such a kind of life, nothing could change that.

For the first few days, he had his own inhibitions in carrying out his duties as a Priest in the temple. Gradually, trained by the old land lord, he became adept at his job. Everyday, he prayed for the welfare and happiness of his family and believed that being Omnipotent, God was sure to take care of them.

The people who came to the temple regularly were taken aback by the kindness of Swaminathan so much so that many of them confided their personal problems in him. As he listened to their woes, Swaminathan realised that he was not alone and that he was in the midst of people who had more heart-rending and poignant stories to tell ; which made his own problems seem trivial........

Severing all his ties, Swaminathan continued to work in the Vinayagar Temple peacefully. Cocooned in his own world, he had never felt more secure. And now, Ramanathan's visit had once again turned his life topsy turvy. His promise to unite him with his family members filled his mind with apprehensions. All these years he had been leading a spiritualistic life bereft of any attachments. Now, he was worried about his future-was it going to be a peaceful one or full of hurdles.

Swaminathan had indeed taken a big step in leaving his family and now joining them back was a giant leap over a chasm. For the rest of the night after Ramanathan left, he kept contemplating about his life, which was going to take a sea change. Ramanathan had in fact kindled his feelings of love and affection towards his family ; which had been lying dormant so far.

Swaminathan met the old man and his wife and conveyed the news to them. He told them that since he had found a new job in Chennai, he had to leave immediately. While the old couple appreciated the fact that he was leaving for better prospects they felt sad at his departure. They had been affectionate towards

Swaminathan and had treated him like a family member. They regretted that there would be no one around to carry out their day to day errands. After blessing him with happiness they told him that they will be missing him a lot.

On Wednesday morning, Swaminathan woke up earlier than usual and started packing up his things. Since he had been leading a frugal life all these years, he was able to stuff his belongings into a small bag. He discarded most of the things that he would have no need for in the future. However he decided to treasure the small religious books the old man had given him. As he was putting them into his bag, he was once again attracted by the small glossy yellow colour book. Six years back, it had changed his mind and cleared all his confusions. It was early dawn and still dark outside. There was plenty of time left for him to reach the temple. Swaminathan decided to while away his time till then by reading this book.

He read the book very slowly page after page as if it held the answers to all the questions in his mind. And when he came to the fag end of the book, he heaved a sigh of great relief. His premonition had indeed been right. For once again the little book helped him ease his mental agony. He read the following sentences over and over again and was touched by it.

The Upanishads do not tell us to be other wordly. They tell us to be part of the perceived world, performing all Earthly and social duties while we simultaneously aspire for spiritual progress. Perform all duties without attachment. Your karma should never be a baggage.

Swaminathan had been weighing the pros and cons of going back to his family. Now, he realised that it was afterall God's will that he return to his family. He considered the little book as God sent ; for once again, it steadied his perturbed mind and removed his restlessness. He was now bent upon joining his family and looked forward to meeting them.

He was not sure about the reception from his wife, but he was confident that Shruthi would welcome him with a open heart. Suddenly, Swaminathan was engulfed with feelings of love for his daughter and wished to see her immediately, no matter what. He had been unlucky and missed watching her grow up. Shruthi would have become a Teenager by now and he did not wish to miss her further. He was yearning to be by her side right away, more than ever.

As the sky was streaked with the first rays of the sun, heralding the beginning of a new dawn, Swaminathan got up and walked swiftly to the temple with rejuvenation. Today was the D-Day - a Turning Point in his life - when a transformation from a spiritualistic life to a temporal life was about to occur. To Swaminathan, this was a great ordeal and he sought God's blessings for facilitating a smooth transition.

While performing the puja that day, he kept looking askance for any sign of Ramanathan. It was Noon and Swaminathan got rather tensed when nobody had turned up. He locked the temple and handed over the keys to the temple authorities and bid good bye to everyone. For the rest of the day, he sat in his room in silence. As the time kept ticking by, Swaminathan was racked with worry. What exactly could be holding Ramanathan ? Why did he not keep his promise ?

For Six long years, Swaminathan had been leading a solitary life. It was only Ramanathan who had brain washed him and explained to him about the happiness one derives from a committed married life despite marital clashes that might arise from time to time. Further, he had reprimanded him for taking life so seriously and asked him to get back to his family. After a long sermon, Ramanathan was successfully able to drive home his point and now Swaminathan was waiting with abated breath to join his family members.

The Twilight was slowly turning into dusk and when no one turned up still, Swaminathan felt deflated. And finally when darkness closed in, his mind was plugged with a volley of questions. Was Shanthi angry with him for deserting her and had she told Ramanathan point blank that she was not willing to see him ? And was this the reason Ramanathan stayed back ; for he did not wish to hurt him by giving a negative reply ?

Swaminathan was getting restless and he could wait no longer. Suddenly, the whole thing seemed ridiculous to him. Why did he need a mediator in the first place? It was his own family that he was going back to. Due to some bad patch of time, he had taken a drastic decision of leaving them. And why was he feeling so nervous about joining them back. After all, his spiritualistic life had taught him to face any hardships in life and also changed him into a subdued person. In fact, whatever be the treatment Shanthi would be meting out to him, he was prepared to face it. This being the case, why was he waiting for Ramanthan's intervention ? Indeed, Ramanathan had been responsible for opening his eyes to the realities of life and now it was time for him to act. Early the next morning, Swaminathan took the first bus that left to Chennai.

When he reached his house, he found it locked. He then started walking to his Mother-In-Law's house hoping to find Shanthi there and became vexed on finding it locked too. Irked by the minor set backs that was holding him from his reunion with his family, Swaminathan caught an auto and went to his aunt's house.

He heaved a sigh of relief on seeing the door wide open. Since there was no one in the vicinity, he went from one room to another looking for his aunt. Finally, he saw her in the backyard drying out the clothes. On seeing Swaminathan, she became dumbfounded. Stopping her work abruptly, she came striding towards him and with a startled expression, she asked, "Swami, where had you been all these years ? Even without telling a word to me, you disappeared all of a sudden. You very well know that you have a special place in my heart. You could have shared your problems with me. Instead, you had cooly run away from your family, leaving them in a lurch. Don't you think that this is a cowardly act ? I still cannot digest the fact that you did this........"

Swaminathan, realizing that his aunt was not going to stop her rambling, interjected smoothly, "well, at that point of time, I had no choice but to leave. Shanthi was turning atrocious day by day and she was getting on my nerves. She started giving vent to her anger by hitting my poor daughter, for no fault of hers. This was turning me wild and I feared that I too would become as rough as my father and do some hurrid thing. Moreover, I did not wish that my daughter grows up in the midst of parent rivalry and so I left. I am now back to take care of her."

His aunt however continued to be relentless and she said, "whatever be the justification you give, I shall never forgive you for having ditched your family like that. Shanthi was in fact too possessive of you and wanted your exclusive love and affection. But this is a common trait among women. Ofcourse, Shanthi has overdone this by exceeding her limits ; trying to keep you under her control. She however does have a soft corner and is not a heartless woman as you seem to think. One fine day, I was shell shocked when she walked into my house crying and asked me if I knew anything about your whereabouts. I had a horrible time in consoling her. She then told me that she really felt sorry for having been harsh with you and promised to behave well when you returned. Even now, she keeps phoning to me from time to time to find out if I had heard anything from you. I would then allay her fears by assuring her that you would come back one day or the other. I feel happy that at last my words have come out true !"

Swaminathan listened to his aunt's reproof without contradicting her and she continuted rattling in favour of Shanthi for long ; all the while berating him. At last, she stood up in a huff and went into get her cell phone to convey the happy news to Shanthi.

When Shanthi heard the news, she let out a whoop of glee, making everyone in the bus turn around to see the source from where it was emanating. Not minding their stares, Shanthi continued speaking with the same fervor ; repeatedly asking his aunt if what she was saying was absolute truth. Finally, convinced that she was not playing any kind of prank on her, she said rather joyfully, "I knew right from the beginning that he would come back one day or the other. I was only not sure when that was going to be. Well, I shall be there within an hour." For the rest of the journey, Shanthi could not sit still for her heart kept racing over the thought of meeting her husband after a gap of six long years.

As Shanthi was sharing the news with everyone, Shruthi was getting much excited too. She could not wait to meet her father and kept pestering her mother all the way as to how long will it be before they reach home.

Leaving Swaminathan in the hall, his aunt entered the kitchen to preapre a feast to celebrate his return. When Swaminathan volunteered to help her in any possible way, she curtly refused and asked him to be ready to welcome his people. Swaminathan ; gearing up himself for a good dressing down from everyone, settled down in front of the TV.

It was Ramanathan who came in first. Flashing a smile at him, he apologised, "I am sorry about not meeting you yesterday as promised. As usual it was due to my poor memory that such a lapse had occurred." Then with a wink, he continued, "however, this morning, when I did not find you either in the temple or in your room, I guessed that you might have come here on your own." His Father-In-Law who joined him shortly butted in, "you don't have to apologize. After all, you get the credit of bringing him back to us. All is well that ends well !" Turning to Swaminathan, he admonished with a rather grim face, "you should have not done this to my daughter. Shanthi is really broken. Afterall, Quarrels between spouses is a common thing and running away from the issue or giving up your life is not the right solution to all the marital blues. One has to make a lot of adjustments in order to lead a happy married life. Your absconding has not affected Shanthi alone but all of us." On seeing his daughter enter, he stopped his tirade ; letting her take over.

When her eyes fell on Swaminathan, words failed her. The moment froze as they stared at each other. It took Shanthi a few seconds to pull herself together before she could even utter a word. She tried to blink several times to stop from crying but all her pent up emotions surfaced and tears sprang up to her eyes. With tears rolling down her cheeks, she asked, "why did you do this to me ? Why did you walk out of my life ?"

Swaminathan did not wish to make a futile attempt in justifying his action. After all, he was aware that he had committed a blunder in his life and was now all set to face the brunt of her anger. He stood there grinning sheepishly at her. Stepping closer to him, she said, "do you know something ? I had been worrying myself sick over you all these years. Now, you owe me an explanation for your dastardly act !"

There was still no response from Swaminathan. His silence only infuriated her further. All of a sudden, she started pounding his chest with her fists ; mustering all her strength. "Tell me why did you run away from me ?", she demanded amidst tears. "Is it wrong for a wife to be too possessive of her husband ? All I wanted was your exclusive love and time for me. Was I asking for too much ?" Come on, answer me as to what did I do to beget such a punishment ?"

Swaminathan continued to stand there silently ; giving her a toothy smile all the while, as he received her blows.

When she did not get any reply from him, she became hysterical and started bawling at him, "you too behaved like your ruthless father, isn't it ? It is all in your genes ! Like your parents who ended their lives leaving you to fend for yourself, you had also left us in the lurch. You are so heartless !"

Swaminathan was least affected by her unruly behaviour. In fact, he only felt pity for her. For he noticed that Shanthi had lost her usual charm and looked so devastated. Probably his separation had cost her emotionally. He tried to placate her agitated mood. Slowly, he held both her hands together in a strong grip to stop her from hitting him further and said, "that's enough Shanthi. Now relax a little. Don't hurt your hands by hitting me so hard. I am extremely sorry for behaving in a wayward manner. I myself never expected these twists and turns in my life. I was so upset by your rudeness and in a total chaos at that time. Leaving you was the only option that made sense to me then." Releasing her hands, he said, "well, I have now come back to live with you and don't smash my heart by being so violent."

His remark made her lips quiver with a smile and as she saw Shruthi and her grandmother walk in to the hall, she started wiping away her tears.

Even before entering the house, Shruthi was able to hear the loud commotion between her parents. She was worried that her mother was yelling at her father as usual. Sadly, she walked up to her and whispered, "Ma, please don't shout at father like this. It is only now that he has returned after so many years. If you show your anger at him, he might leave us all once again."

Swaminathan's face lit up with a luminous smile on seeing his daughter, who had grown up so big. He stood there admiring her for a while and then dragging her close to him, he asked, "is this my little princess ?" Shruthi stood there grinning shyly at her father. Giving her a bear hug, he said, "to tell you the truth young lady, it was just for your happiness that I left in the first place. I did not want you to grow up in the midst of parent rivalry or get beaten frequently by your mother on account of me. I am now back to take care of you and promise never to leave you again."

Bubbling with excitement, Shruthi said, "you are indeed right daddy ! After you left, mother was very kind to me and did not hit me even once. However, I felt sorry for her because she would get into a sullen mood very often and I would have a tough time in comforting her." Trying to appease Shanthi, he said, "see what your daughter says. She enjoyed your love and affection ! May be this separation was a blessing to all of us. Shruthi was able to grow up in a peaceful atmosphere and it also lifted me spiritually ; enriching me with the capacity of tolerance. And perhaps it has also softened my beloved wife a little !"

His words only cut through her like a knife and she started screaming at him once again, "you call this a blessing ? One fine day, you cooly walk out, shattering my life and you call this a blessing ?" Tears started afresh and while Swaminathan was trying to pacify her, his aunt barged into the hall.

Greeting everyone with a smile, she announced, "I have cooked a sumptuous fare to celebrate Swaminathan's return." Ushering them in to the dining hall, she said, "all of you please come and have your meals now for it is already past lunch hour." Further holding Shanthi's hand, she said with a smile, "see, my words have turned out to be true. Swaminathan is back. Now, stop worrying and start living a happy life with your husband !"

Ramanathan got up immediately and excused himself. "Thanks for your invitation but I am afraid I will not be able to join. I had promised my wife that I will be having lunch with her and she will be waiting for me. I shall now take leave of all of you."

He then turned to Shanthi and asked with an edge of triumph in his voice, "haven't I solved all your problems now ? Well, go and enjoy the feast along with your husband." With a twinkle in his eyes, he added, "you may reserve your fights for a little longer until you reach home. It would be apt to mention here about a Chinese proverb which goes like this - the tongue is but three inches long, yet it can kill a man six feet high. Stop lashing out at Swaminathan and take good care of him ; for he is a man with a heart of gold." Shanthi stood there in silence, giving him a smile of thanks.

Shruthi sat down beside her father and kept chattering all the while ; updating him about the various events that had occurred during his absence. Swaminathan was all ears to his daughter's babbling. Finally when Shruthi told him about her rude Principal who refused to give her transfer certificate because her father did not accompany her, he responded immediately to her grievance by telling that he would meet her principal the next day itself and get the required transfer certificate. With happiness writ large over her face, Shruthi said, "you have come back at the right time daddy. I can now join the new school along with my best friend." She then started to brief him about the reasons for choosing Saranya as her best friend.

That night when Shanthi was alone with her husband, she said, "I know I have nagged you enough; stretching your patience beyond your tolerance limit, but is this the way you punish me ?"

"Well, I already told you that I did not mean to ditch you. Our life fell apart and it was all God's doing. How can we know God's love if we never have any problems in our lives ? Only if you had been in the deepest valley would you ever know the magnificience of the highest mountains."

"Well, I too sought solace from divine intervention and believed that my firm faith in Him would bring you back one day or the other."

Swaminathan took out a string of jasmine flowers from his bag and handing it over to Shanthi said, "well, I have already agreed that I am in the fault. Why don't we forget the past as a bad dream and start our life afresh."

Shanthi immediately dug her face into the flowers and inhaling its fragrance said, "how coolly you ask me to forget the whole thing ! You know something ? My life had been a hell of a storm without you. All these years, I could think of nothingelse but you !"

Popping into the room from nowhere, Shruthi said, "and daddy's return is like seeing the rainbow after the storm." Without even waiting to listen to her mother's comment, she left the room as swiftly as she came. Shruthi's rejoinder lit up her face with a smile. Continuing to sniff the flowers, she glanced up at her husband. "Your little princess had been eavesdropping our conversation." She said with a giggle.

Suddenly, Swaminathan was overwhelmed with a feeling of affection for his wife. Love squeezed his heart. "For how long you intend to keep your face thrust into the flowers ? Put that on your hair and come over here." He chided her lovingly.

After doubly checking that the door was bolted, Swaminathan returned to his wife with open arms. Shanthi trembled with excitement as she stepped into her husband's arms. He put both arms around her and pulled her as close as she could come. As he cupped her face and gently placed a kiss on her cheeks, a huge grin spread across her face. She pressed her face against his chest with joy blooming through her. With her husband close to her, she felt much stronger.

Swaminathan too felt that he had finally come home for he had Shanthi in his arms now. There is no turning back !

Index